REDVERS CO

C000147847

Roscoe Howells

GOMER

First Impression—1994

ISBN 1 85902 117 4

© Roscoe Howells

Printed by
J. D. Lewis & Sons Ltd., Gomer Press, Llandysul Dyfed

To the memory of
OZ

CONTENTS

Chapter 1

AN IDEA IS DISCUSSED

They took little notice of the old fox. As Ranter said, there was never any fool like an old fool.

Dark red old Redvers was. Darker than any of the other City foxes, most of whom were varying shades of yellowish brown. But the most distinctive feature about him was the tip of his tail. Whereas many of the foxes had either a white tip or a black tip to the tail, Redvers had a big white tip, but with a fine black ring round it.

They all knew how set he was in his ways, so there was no point in trying to argue with him. Always it was the same old story. They had never had it so good, and if the younger ones could know the half of what he knew from the stories handed down in his family, they would be thankful for the good life and all the benefits of living in the City where no man's hand was against them.

'Do you not understand,' Redvers said, 'that the people here put out food for us in their gardens and watch us from their windows? There are no hounds to chase us, no horrid steel traps, and no man would dream of putting down poison for us. Nobody here even owns a gun. Do you not appreciate such a life of great comfort?'

'Comfort?' Ranter said. 'What about the machines that have moved in and destroyed the best dens we ever had? What about that then? Where's the comfort in that? And what about all the horrid cars and that, with their fumes and smells?'

Even Redvers knew that to be true. The humans had started to build a great new road of concrete right through the heartland of the City where the foxes had had their homes for generations. Whole rows of houses had been knocked down and there was devastation, with bright lights everywhere. No peace from the clatter of the great machines, no privacy, and no longer any food from where the houses had once been.

Redvers had often heard it said that, long ago, where they now lived had been fields and woods, until the City had grown so big that their territory had become part of it. So the foxes just adapted their customs, stayed on where their ancestors had been for generations before them, and started to lead the easier life which came with City living. And this had turned out to be so good that word somehow or other reached the foxes way out in the far off parts of the country and some of them had moved into the City. Come one, come all. There was room for everybody.

The present crisis, Redvers believed, could just as easily be overcome. They could adapt again, although it was perhaps a little inconvenient for the time being.

'That's not all, though,' chipped in young Bushtail. 'We're so crowded here now we have to fight for our food. And if we can't get to the nice bits left in the gardens we have to go scavenging around the dustbins.'

'Exactly,' said Ranter, who knew all the answers. 'That's just exactly it as a matter of fact. And now there have been so many complaints that the humans have made a law that dustbins must be made secure and some of us are reduced to rooting round the rubbish heaps, until we're no better off than any country fox.'

'Brothers,' Redvers said, 'don't be fooled. Don't be misled. There was an old, old fox in my family, way, way back, and he was one of the first litter born in this City to one of the first vixens to move in from the country. And he was sly and cunning beyond the average run of foxes and made

10

sure the stories were told and remembered and handed down to us who have come after.'

'What's that got to do with it?' Ranter demanded to know, suspicion written all over his sly face.

'What's it got to do with it?' Redvers snapped. ''I'll tell you what it's got to do with it. Out in the country there are hounds. There are steel traps. There are guns. There is poison. In the winter when the ground is frozen nobody puts out food in their gardens. There are few dustbins. I've heard that no longer do the hens roam free even, and farmers keep their sheep in big sheds at lambing time. Life is hard, my friends. Hard indeed for them in the country.'

'Redvers, old man,' young Bushtail said, 'you just don't have a clue. You're living in the past.'

'And what do you know about it, anyway, you young upstart?'

'I'll tell you what I know about it,' young Bushtail said, 'and maybe it's a bit more up-to-date than all that stuff you've been trying to give us. My father was born in the City wasn't he? And his mother was killed by a car, and so my father was picked up when he was small and the humans fed him and looked after him. And then they took him out into the country and turned him loose.'

'Well?' Redvers said. He always said 'well' just like that when he couldn't think of anything else to say.

'Well what?' said young Bushtail showing no respect for his elders. 'I'll tell you ''well what''. My father said he's heard the stories you and the old ones have been passing on for years, but he found it wasn't like that at all. To start with there are people trying to stop the hounds and there are no longer any steel traps. In fact, he said there are now so many humans in the countryside saying God bless the little foxes that all the country foxes are saying they've never had it so good. He talked to many of them. And being brought up by humans he came to understand what they were saying. That's how he came to be called Herman. He was trying to explain he'd been brought up by a human and they thought he was saying Herman.'

'And what about the guns?' Redvers demanded.

'Guns?' young Bushtail showed his teeth in a contemptuous grin. 'Guns? You're joking. About the only humans with guns now are the criminals who go around shooting each

11

other. Father said that any human entitled to own a gun had to keep it in a case with so many locks on it that by the time they could get it out even the most stupid fox in the country could be two fields away at no more that a gentle trot.'

'Stupid did you say? Country foxes stupid?' Redvers was plainly shocked.

'Yes, stupid,'young Bushtail said. 'My father said that the country foxes are so stupid they don't know they're born.'

'Then what did he come back here for?'

'I'll tell you that as well. He came back here to pass on the good word. He wanted his family to know what the good life was like, way out there over the far hill. Ever since I was born he's been telling me and waiting for me to pass the message on.'

'Then why isn't he here to tell us about it now?'

'Fair question, old fox. Fair question. I'm glad you asked it. He's out and about spreading the good word. This isn't the only part of the City that's been affected, you know. But you wouldn't know about that, would you? You may be contented, but there's some as wants a better life.'

'All right,' said Ranter. 'That's enough of this bickering. We'll call a meeting and decide what's best to do.'

'What d'you mean?' Redvers said. 'Best to do what?'

'Well, we've got to do something, haven't we? Maybe we'd better move out.'

'Move out? To the country you mean? Move out to the country?'

'Of course. There's been enough talk about it often enough and long enough. So now all this is happening around here it's as good a time as any. Get away to a bit of fresh air and the quiet life.'

'You don't need a meeting to decide that,' Redvers said. 'Anybody who wants to go can just go.'

'That's not it,' Ranter said. 'We need to be enough of us to have our own settlement. Make sure things are run properly, the same as here. That is the key issue.'

'Apart from that,' young Bushtail said, 'we need to have a meeting fairly soon to decide who's to mate with which vixens this season.'

Not for the first time the meeting was not all that young Bushtail could have wished.

A few vixens had put in an appearance out of curiosity to see what was going on, but nobody would be taking much notice of them as yet. Any views they were likely to express would be of little consequence. Their function in life would come at mating time.

The theory was that it must be decided in committee which dog fox should have which vixen. That, so they said, had been agreed and set out in the constitution years ago, and it had seemed to be a good idea at first and had worked well, and it had ensured that there had always been a good strain of healthy foxes. That was the sure way to survival. But young Bushtail was beginning to see for himself that it wasn't working out that way at all these days. He certainly wasn't getting his fair share. Ranter saw to that.

This time was no exception. It was the first item young Bushtail wanted them to discuss, but Ranter said, 'Point of order. The urgency of a move to the country must take precedence. The issue of mating and choice of vixens will be dealt with by the usual sub-committee.'

Before young Bushtail could think up a quick answer Ranter had called on young Bushtail's father to give a report on the latest developments as he had seen them on his recent travels in the City. And since young Bushtail had just been shouting the odds about how clever and wise his father was, and how much he knew, he thought it might not be very good tactics to interrupt too strongly at this point.

'I have already had a word with Brother Herman,' Ranter said, 'and I venture to suggest that you will find what he has to tell you very disturbing. Yes, very disturbing indeed. I can understand the sort of thoughts exercising the mind of young Bushtail. Oh yes, very natural. Natural indeed. But what Brother Herman has to tell us affects our very existence. It is a key issue. Yes indeed. Our very existence.'

There must have been more than twenty foxes there altogether and most of them would be reporting back to their own communities.

Herman cleared his throat, looked rather important, and said, 'As you know, Comrades, I have some small knowledge of life in the country. I was brought up there. And things have changed out of all recognition from what you may have had reason to believe. But I've told many of you about this previously. You know how I feel. I came back

13

here out of regard for all of you to tell you about the good life that is waiting for you out there beyond the hill. I make no secret of the fact. I have believed for a long time that it would be a good thing to move back into the country. We are so superior in intelligence to the foxes of the countryside, and we have learned so much from living as we do with our affairs being properly ordered and managed, that we would be at a great advantage. And now I am more convinced than ever that it is time to move.'

Here, Herman paused and sniffed the wind. He was conscious of a slight restlessness amongst a few of his listeners, but he was nothing if not a convincing orator, and he was skilled at creating the right effect.

'Oh, yes,' he smiled, 'I know what you're thinking. You've heard it all before. Some of you believe me, and some of you don't. That is your prerogative. Even in our well-ordered society a fox is still free to think his own thoughts. But it is no longer a matter of opinion. It has become a matter of vital and overriding necessity. It is now imperative for us to move if we are to survive.'

He paused again, but there was no further show of dissent. Use a long word like prerogative and even the most truculent of the younger ones would think twice about showing any impatience.

'Now listen carefully, my friends,' Herman said, 'for you may not have the chance again. As you may know, I have been on the move trying to spread the good word. Not only telling our Comrades throughout this great City about the good life out there beyond the hills, although that was my chief purpose at first. But I was also anxious to assess the current position for myself. And that position, Comrades, is far, far more serious than anything you or I could have believed possible. You know how disturbed many of us have been about what is happening around here with the great machines and the bright lights as they clatter about and shine all through the night, and we have been worried about the serious implications of it.'

That was another good word, Herman said to himself. But here old Redvers interrupted and said, 'So tell us, Brother Herman, what are the implications?'

'The implications,' Herman said, 'are very simple, Comrade Redvers. We shall have to move.'

14

A young yellow coloured vixen, with black-tipped ears, white tip to her tail and white underparts, but with a pronounced black cross over her shoulders, made so bold as to say, 'And are there not many other suitable places in this great City where we may live as comfortably and as easily as we have always done here?'

Herman looked round with a superior air. 'Yes,' he said, 'many other places where we could have lived. Once upon a time. But I say could have lived, and once upon a time, because not any longer. Not only is the same thing happening all over this great City, but worse things are happening. Much worse. Whole communities of foxes are on the move looking for fresh quarters. And what are the implications? I repeat the word and I use it advisedly. Implications. And I will tell you what the implications are. There is not enough room for all of us. And not only can those of us with vision see it for ourselves, but the humans have realised it.'

'The humans?' Redvers said.

'Yes, the humans,' Herman said, and waited for the significance of his words to sink in. 'The humans. With so many foxes on the move looking for new areas in which to settle, the humans have started to send out vans and have already caught untold numbers of our Comrades and taken them away we know not where. So those are the implications, and you must answer the question for yourselves. Do you wish to stay here and be taken away in a van, or do you opt for freedom and the good life in the woods and the fields of our ancestors? The living, Comrades, which is our birthright out there in the countryside, where the foxes are generations behind the times and where we could lead a life such as our ancestors never dreamed of. A life of freedom and food in abundance, but where the hand of man would no longer be against us as in days of old. The time has come, friends. We cannot put off making a decision any longer.'

Chapter 2

THE PLAN IS MADE

Oratory such as they had heard from Herman that night was more than enough to convince those who had already been considering the possibilities. Their instinct for self-preservation was strong. It was true that there were now many foxes all over the City. But who knew, and who could say, how many?

It was also true about the vans going round to carry away foxes which were being captured as they wandered bewildered looking for new places to settle. Several delegates had confirmed that part of Herman's story. With all the great machines clattering about, and the bright lights shining everywhere all through the nights so that the humans could go on working, the foxes were having to show themselves in ever increasing numbers, and maybe it had come as a surprise to the humans to realise how many foxes there really were. It was altogether a time of great upheaval. This question of the vans was the last straw.

By the time the delegates had reported back, and another meeting had been called, it was well past autumn and they were into the mating season. Young Bushtail was none too pleased with the vixen allocated to him by Ranter's committee.

Originally, it was said, when the constitution had been drawn up, the idea had been that, by wise selection of the

16

right mates, the stock would remain strong and healthy. But, with the only selecting being done to suit their own personal tastes by the likes of Ranter and his cronies, it was hardly surprising that some of them had become a pretty weedy and scruffy looking crowd. Young Bushtail didn't think much of Ranter. One day his own turn would come. One day.

All through the autumn there were reports of the vans taking away more captured foxes. One of them was the vixen Bushtail had covered, but that didn't worry Bushtail. As he said to one of his mates, there had been nothing much about her to attract a healthy young fox. Come the spring, at least he would have no young cubs to worry about. And the spring was what most of them had in mind these days.

The weather had turned cold, and there was snow on the ground, so with all the disruption it was a hard winter for the foxes. Even Herman had to admit it would be an act of folly to set off at such a time for what would be to all of them except himself unknown country and an almost new way of life.

The litters of cubs would be born in February, and it would take some weeks to teach them how to fend for themselves. So Herman advised that they should think in terms of setting off in the spring. On the other hand they must not delay any longer than was really necessary because they would need to travel before the days had started to lengthen too much, and they began to plan accordingly.

From five different communities the foxes would come, from all over the City, and there would also be three, or perhaps four, whole families. These would be from the first vixens to cub. The idea was that the first foxes to arrive in the country should see for themselves what conditions were like, and in due course report back to any others who might think of following.

As the time approached, however, there came, too, an awareness that the great exodus might not be without its considerable practical difficulties. Already there were more than thirty foxes in the official party, and who could guess how many might tag on uninvited?

As old Redvers had said at the start, 'You don't need a meeting to decide to move into the country. Anybody who wants to go can just go.' That's what he had said, and there

17

were plenty of those who were willing to listen to him, whatever young Bushtail may have had to say about his old-fashioned ideas. In fact, it was Redvers who had pointed out one of the most hazardous parts of the whole move.

'Have you stopped to think what it's going to be like?' he said. 'How many will you be? For all you know now, you could finish up with more than fifty of you on the move.'

Ranter sat on his haunches with his bushy tail curled round him, and his big ears were well forward. He was thinking.

'Good point, Comrade,' he said. 'Good point indeed. A very good point I think. What does Brother Herman think?'

'It should not be too difficult,' Herman said, 'but fair's fair. It was wise of Brother Redvers to mention it. Very wise. That number of us on the move in strange territory could attract the attention of the humans and arouse their suspicions, and 'twould no doubt be difficult to conceal everybody.'

'We shall only move by night,' one of the foxes said.

'Quite so,' Herman said, 'quite so. But in the country there are always dogs about the farmyards to bark and rouse the humans. One fox can hide where fifty couldn't. Likewise we shall leave tracks. And we must not arouse suspicions.'

'You will also need to eat,' observed Redvers, who was pleased to have been taken more seriously at last, and who thought it was good of Herman to have acknowledged his wisdom. It also had to be admitted that Herman did indeed know something about the countryside.

'Point of order,' said Ranter. 'A mere detail. That has been discussed in committee and plans on this key issue have been made accordingly. I give you my word for that.'

'Who the hell would take your word for anything?' young Bushtail muttered, but not loud enough for Ranter to hear. But some of the others heard and couldn't suppress a snigger. Young Bushtail was not the only one who sensed that Ranter was bidding to set himself up as being wiser than Herman, and Bushtail felt that old Redvers had been decent enough to show such an interest in a scheme of which he was known to disapprove. At least he should be given credit for that.

'That's enough bickering,' Ranter said. 'We must devise a plan. It's a key issue and the committee will consider it.'

'No need for a committee meeting,' Redvers said. 'It's

simple. Don't all move out together. No more than half-a-dozen or so to set off with Herman, and travel hard for one night. Lie up for one day, and on the second night let one trusted Comrade return. The next night he will guide another group to follow Herman who will move on and send another trusted Comrade back to lead the others and so on and so on. How many nights' journey does Herman think he will need to reach wherever he plans to go? I suppose he has somewhere in mind?'

'Indeed,' said Herman. 'Yes indeed. Very much so. It is a great wood. The finest and fairest, as well as the hugest I ever did see. A huge wood indeed.'

'And how many nights' travel?' asked Ranter.

Herman sniffed the air with his wet nose, as he always did when he was thinking.

'If all goes well,' he said, 'we should do it in the space of one moon. It will take longer, of course, if we have to do it in stages waiting for each group to catch up with the one ahead. But it will be worth it.'

'You think so?' Ranter said.

A sly grin came over Herman's face. 'Very much so. If fifty of us managed to turn up at the same time the local foxes might start asking questions. A few at a time and we can prepare the way for others. Apart from the big wood there are many other lovely woods within a night's travel. We can spread out. Yes, there is much to be said for it.'

'Point of order,' Ranter said. 'Time is important now, so that's agreed.'

Chapter 3

DEPARTURE

Spring came at last. Slowly at first, almost imperceptibly, and then with something of a rush. In the parks the snowdrops had given way to the daffodils nodding in the breeze, and the primroses flourished in the moist and shady corners. There, too, in the soft earth, there were easier pickings of beetles, slugs and many another tasty morsel, field mice and the occasional egg or young from the nests of the birds foolish enough to have built too near to the ground. Some of the waterfowl were incredibly foolish in the way they made their nests round the edges of the lakes in the parks to provide rich fare from time to time. Maybe they were first-year birds that had not yet learned their lesson. Up in the branches, the pigeons cooed gently. Their forbears had learned their lesson long, long ago.

Early in April, before the bluebells came, there were three consecutive nights of ground frost. Herman turned his wet nose to the wind and knew there would follow a long spell of good weather, and the word was to prepare for the great adventure.

A few nights before they were due to set out young Bushtail happened to meet up with Redvers near a dustbin in a back alley, behind a row of terraced houses which had so far escaped demolition by the big machines.

They exchanged the usual pleasantries, and then young Bushtail said, 'It was good of you to offer such good advice on our move to the country. Especially when it's so well known you're not in favour of it.'

'Not at all,' Redvers said. 'You are all my people, and I'm concerned for you. It was good of Herman to speak so kindly of my opinion, and good of him to listen to my suggestions.'

'Not just good of him, Redvers. Sensible.'

'You think so?'

'I'm sure of it.'

A light came on in a window near them, a door banged, and there was the sound of human voices. Redvers and young Bushtail froze with their ears forward. For long minutes they moved not a muscle. At last the door banged again and the light went out. Still they made no move. Then a cat jumped up onto the wall halfway along the alley and somewhere in the distance a dog barked. Way beyond that the great machines were clattering and the bright lights were shining.

''Twill be nice to be out from here and away from this lot,' young Bushtail said.

'Sometimes,' said Redvers, 'I think maybe you have a point.'

'Then why not come with us?'

'I'm too old. Too set in my ways.'

'Nonsense. You're wise. You've seen so much of life.'

'Yes, Bushtail. Much indeed. But not of life in the country.'

'I know, I know. You live in the past. But you still have all a fox's cunning.'

'Too true I have. And I saw through our friend Ranter long ago.'

'He's no friend of mine.'

'I know that, young Bushtail. He's no friend of anybody's apart from Comrade Ranter himself.'

'Did you see the miserable little vixen he and his so-called committee allocated to me this year?'

'Not much to look at was she?'

'A wretched poor creature. She was hot enough under the tail, but that's all you could say for her.'

'Did I hear she was one of those who'd been caught and sent off in a van?''

'Yes, poor thing. But it'll leave me free in the spring with no cubs to bother about. We have to think of ourselves in this life.'

'Like Ranter.'

21

'Aye, like Ranter. You said yourself you can see through him all right. Why don't you come with us? You could give plenty of good advice.'

'Not about the country.'

'But you know about characters like Ranter.'

'Maybe so. But I'm worried about it all. Herman was brought up by humans, so he came to understand their language and what they were saying. But there's more to it than that. He was probably with the sort of humans who think all foxes are lovely creatures. But don't forget that my family are well-known for the stories that have been handed down since time out of mind. I'm still willing to believe what the old ones said. And they knew only too well about the humans. I don't suppose they'll all be like the ones who brought up Herman.'

'But he said, didn't he, that the country foxes are all stupid?'

'Yes, he said that. But who's to say what is stupid and what isn't? They may be stupid according to our way of thinking, but we've evolved a whole new way of life suitable to living in the City. The foxes in the country will know what's best for them. You can be sure of that. Yes, quite sure.'

'Redvers,' young Bushtail said, 'come with us. If it's only to keep an eye on Comrade Ranter.'

Redvers grinned. 'On the key issues, you mean?'

'Him and his key issues. The only key issue he knows about is picking the best vixens in season for himself and his buddies.'

Redvers turned his nose to the wind and thought for a while.

'Maybe,' he said. 'Maybe I could come with you to see what it's like and then come back here to end my days in peace once you're all settled. Yes, maybe I could think about that. Yes indeed. Maybe I could think about it.'

As time went by Bushtail came round more and more to the idea that maybe old Redvers wasn't a bad sort after all, and that he had perhaps agreed to move with the others out of a genuine regard for them and in order to be of some help. Bushtail was beginning to think that his father was possibly not as smart as he had always made himself out to be. The

22

more Bushtail saw of Ranter, the more he wondered why Herman could be working so closely with him.

They had set out on the first stage of their journey soon after sundown on a clear, crisp evening, when the birds in the park had scarcely settled for the night. By the time it was dark, the foxes were still in familiar territory.

Eight of them there were, and two of the four from other communities were vixens. Bushtail couldn't help but wonder whether Ranter had designs on them for next mating season, for they weren't bad lookers. One of them was the pretty yellow coloured vixen who had been so bold as to ask the question at the meeting. Bushtail thought that could be interesting. Maybe he would keep his eye on her. He had one or two old scores to settle with Ranter.

Herman had calculated that it would take at least two nights travelling before they could expect to reach the City suburbs, and Ranter had said that, if one fox went back to collect and guide a second party, and one remained to wait for them, that would leave just six to press on ahead to the next point somewhere out in the country. Herman said he thought this was excellent planning.

They passed many places near to where the great machines were clattering and the bright lights were shining but, because of this, there were many foxes on the move, and their own presence attracted little attention. Bearing in mind the talk of the dreaded vans, they kept well in the shadows and moved with extra caution. The grey dawn was breaking when they found a deserted and derelict building, with brambles and a profusion of nettles growing all round it, and a murky stream crawling sluggishly beside it. Ranter said it would be an ideal spot to rest and to conceal themselves throughout the day, and Herman agreed with him. No doubt there would be a sufficiency of food to be found before they moved on the following evening, and it would be a splendid posting station to await the arrival of the next contingent. Apart from any frogs there may be, and no doubt a profusion of either rats or mice, there were more than enough houses for there to be dustbins and rubbish in the gardens to provide the sources of food with which they were familiar.

The next thing was to decide who would go back and guide the next group, and who would wait for them whilst six of them went on ahead. It was at this point that Ranter decided it was necessary to convene a meeting.

In no time at all he had launched into one of his pompous speeches on key issues and the importance of the constitution, and Herman was agreeing with him.

'Before another dawn,' Herman said, 'some of us will be near to the new land we seek and we must be ever conscious of the civilised ways we bring with us. The country foxes are slow-witted, foolish in many respects, and backward beyond belief. They have old-fashioned ideas about pleasing themselves and living as they have always lived, so as Comrade Ranter has stressed we must safeguard our constitution. That may not always be easy when we find ourselves in new surroundings which will be strange to all of you.'

Herman cleared his throat, and Redvers and Bushtail exchanged knowing glances. Then Herman reminded them at length of his great knowledge of the countryside and the humans, which he had acquired as the result of his early up-bringing, and spoke in glowing terms of the vast opportunities which were waiting for them 'out there.'

Then, lowering his voice, he said, 'Some of the native foxes may not much care for our way of life, but our constitution can serve us just as well in the country areas as it always has in the City.'

'That sounds all fine and large,' Redvers said, 'but we may find our needs are different in the country areas.'

'No such thing, old chap. It's all a question of progress. That was why our constitution was drawn up long ago.'

'What does this constitution say? Who drew it up? When was it adopted? And what does it say?'

'Point of order,' Ranter interpolated. 'We cannot go into the question of the constitution at this moment in time.' Then he launched into a longwinded spiel concerning the details of which fox would go back to guide the next group, and who would go on and who would come back, which made it all sound most bewildering.

'All the way,' he concluded, 'we shall be moving in separate groups with trusted Comrades moving back and forth between us to keep in touch until we have all arrived at our wonderful destination. All that has already been decided and agreed in principle. Now we must work out every little detail.'

The four foxes from other communities immediately started to ask questions and argue with each other, with the two vixens having enough to say for ten, and Ranter had no further need to talk about the constitution.

Chapter 4

FIRST HALT

The great machines were still clattering away, the noise mingling with the more familiar daytime sounds of the City, but the bright lights had dimmed and a warm spring sun was struggling to break through the pall of smoke and the haze which hung above the factory chimneys and the roof-tops. Bushtail slept but fitfully in a sheltered corner he had found behind the bole of a gnarled elder tree. His coat had shades of black, accentuating his white underparts, and a black stripe ran down his spine. His tail, black-tipped, was curled round over his nose, one ear forward and one back. He was conscious of Redvers' approach long before the old fox spoke.

'You sleep lightly, young Bushtail,' he said.

'It's our nature, Redvers.'

'Not the way you've been sleeping since dawn. I've been watching you.'

Bushtail eased himself into a sitting position.

'And why weren't you sleeping yourself?'

'For the same reason that you sleep so lightly even for a fox. I think we have the same misgivings. We do not trust Comrade Ranter.'

'That is also our nature, Redvers. Don't ever trust anybody. Do you trust Herman?'

'I think not,' Redvers said, 'even though he's your father.'

'And I agree with you. The fact that he's my father means nothing to him or me.'

'And that is the nature of us foxes, too.'

Since ever the move to the country had been first suggested, young Bushtail had observed much, and he and Redvers had come to understand each other. At least they had in common their suspicion of Ranter.

'I don't like it,' Redvers said. 'I don't like it at all. But I'm glad you said last night that you'd go on with them to the next resting place.'

'You think it is the right thing to do?'

'Absolutely.'

'I'm glad to hear you say that. You see, I had listened to Herman's talk and all the wonderful stories of life in the country, and maybe they're all true. But when you see him so close to Ranter you start to wonder.'

'And what are you wondering, young Bushtail?'

'That I don't know. But the same as you I expect. I don't like it.'

Redvers raised his nose in the air and his ears were well forward. Then he said, 'Everything is very still at the moment.'

'What's on your mind, Redvers?'

'Suppose the pair of them had some idea of going on ahead on their own. What would you think of that?'

'No. I don't think so. Right from the start, remember, Ranter's been on about the need to have a large enough number to make our own settlement and run things our own way.'

'Indeed,' Redvers said. 'And that means his way. He's power crazy. But he needs Herman as an ally because Herman knows something of the ways of the country. Or so Herman says.'

'You still have doubts about that, don't you?'

'Yes, I do. The stories have been handed down in my family. And the old timers were not fools.'

'Even so, I don't think Ranter would have any idea for them to set off on their own. He'd be too smart for that.'

'Maybe so,' Redvers said, 'but you can be sure of one thing. If it ever suited him he'd go without a thought for any of the others.' Then he grinned and turned a sly look towards his young confidante as he said,

27

'The Ranter fox I do not trust,
Though what I say may be unjust.
Yet still I say, and say I must,
The Ranter fox I do not trust.'

'Indeed,' said Bushtail, 'you're wise there. But I still can't see why he and Herman would want to set off on their own. What benefit could that be to them, Redvers?'

'How do I know? Perhaps it's only a foolish thought on my part which has grown from my deep-rooted suspicion. Our nature, young Bushtail, as you rightly say. Even so, I'm glad you're going on ahead with them.'

'Maybe I had such thoughts in my head when I said I would go with them.'

'And who will come back here to act as guide to the next party?'

'That,' said Bushtail, 'is a good question, old man. They're strangers to us. But in case anything goes wrong, I was wondering whether I could perhaps leave some scent along the way. Do you think that would be any good? Maybe I could get the others to do the same.'

'As I have been doing ever since we set out,' Redvers showed his teeth in a sly grin.

'You're a cunning old fox, aren't you?'

'I've survived, young Bushtail. I've survived. I've heard many a story handed down in our family of how our ancestors survived in the country through leaving messages by scent. Nowadays, living here in the City, it hasn't been necessary. The only time young foxes do it now is for playing games. It's been all so different here from what I was always told it was like in the country.'

Night was falling, and the daytime noises of the City were beginning to die, but the bright lights had come on and the great machines were still clattering, when Ranter convened another of his interminable meetings. The purpose, he said, was to decide who should remain as a link, and who should return to the City to collect the next contingent and guide them this far.

'I've thought of that,' Redvers cut in. 'There's no need to leave any fox here. I can return to the City and find my way back here tomorrow night with the next group.'

28

'Are you sure you will know your way to this exact spot again?' Ranter asked.

'Well, if I can't, there wouldn't be much point in leaving anybody here.'

'That's true, I suppose.'

'And what's more,' Redvers said, 'I reckon I know the City as well as most. Yes, I'll find my way all right. The gate-posts and the very pavements themselves will speak to me.'

Here he gave Bushtail a sly wink, and Bushtail consoled himself by thinking that, even if old Redvers was a bit of a stick-in-the-mud, he was no fool.

'I rely on you to send a trusted Comrade back to lead us forward.'

'Indeed. Most important. I agree with you entirely,' Ranter said. And before he could say any more, Redvers said, 'Good. Then I suggest you send Rudyard. His family are well-known to me and I know them to be reliable.'

'Oh! And how can you be sure that Brother Rudyard will be agreeable to undertake such an important mission?'

'Because I've asked him, and we've talked over some of the details.'

'Oh,' Ranter said again, looking somewhat taken aback at the thought of anyone but himself making suggestions and important decisions. 'Is this so, Brother Rudyard?' he asked.

Rudyard stared back at Ranter in no way disconcerted. A bright-eyed fox he was, even redder in the coat than Redvers, and certainly redder than any of the City foxes, with decidedly white underparts, black at his feet and the back of his ears, and with a white tip to his tail.

'You're not from our community I believe?' Ranter said.

'No, I ain't,' said Rudyard. 'But I knows some of your lot. An' some of ours is just as keen to get out of here an' into the country as all the rest.'

'Do you know this area where we are now?'

''Course I knows it. Knows everywhere. Came here once when we was kicked out of where we was an' went lookin' for a place.'

'And do you think you'll be able to find your way back here tomorrow night on your own?'

'Listen, mate,' Rudyard said, 'I ain't still wet behind the ears. An' how much more time you wantin' to waste wiv a lot o' gab? 'Tis night already an' we wants to be on the move.'

Bushtail could not help but smile to himself to hear the great Ranter being spoken to with such familiarity and truculence.

'Now then, mate,' Rudyard said to Herman, who had been looking on with marked disapproval, 'you're supposed to know where we're goin'. Ain't it about time to get movin'?'

Herman looked at Ranter as if for guidance, and Ranter held his wet nose to the gentle breeze that had now started to ripple such growth as there was.

'Yes, indeed,' Ranter said. 'It is indeed time to move. We shall await your coming three nights hence, Comrade Redvers.'

'I think not, Brother,' said Redvers. 'My first duty will be to see all the foxes by stages as far as this, and then safely out into the country. Before the moon has waned I shall hope to join you.'

'As you wish,' Ranter said, again obviously displeased at not having given the orders. 'I suppose you will come eventually?'

'If all goes well, I shall join you one day with the last group. Whether I shall stay I don't know.'

And then, with a last knowing look at Bushtail, he melted into the shadows.

Bushtail experienced a sense of loss and much apprehension to see Redvers go, but it cheered him to know that this character, Rudyard, was also in Redvers' confidence. And it was even better to see the way he had spoken to Ranter and Herman. He would miss old Redvers, but it looked as if there was at least one fox who might be a useful ally. And so it was that, as the seven foxes moved off, Bushtail kept close to Rudyard.

They had travelled but a short distance when Bushtail saw Rudyard rub the back of his brush against a lamp-post. Rudyard knew that Bushtail had seen him and said, 'Did Redvers tell you, mate?'

'Sure he did,' Bushtail said.

'That's it then. We're in this togevver. You make sure you mark some places as well. An' you needn't let them uvvers see you. I'll watch out for 'em all on the way back, so I'll know your smell. An' make sure you leaves some good marks for me when you moves on tomorrer night in case anyffink goes wrong. I'll need all the messages you can leave.'

Well, as old Redvers had said, the only time young foxes used their scent glands these days was for playing games, but this was no game. This was for real. There was no knowing how serious the nights, and the days, ahead of them might be.

Chapter 5

MOVING ON

Journeying on as they were into the unknown, Bushtail found it a great comfort to have the cheerful and self-confident Rudyard to talk to, and to exchange ideas and experiences with him.

Rudyard had, he said, spent his younger days in the market area of the City where the living was good. There were plenty of scraps there for the taking, and much of it was good meat and fish. Eventually, though, one winter when the snow was on the ground, some fool had overdone it and bitten his way into a shed packed with dressed turkeys. Several other foxes had followed and they had had a tremendous feast. The consequences from the humans, however, had been bitter and prolonged, many foxes had died in agony from poison, and it had no longer been safe to live in that area. He knew some foxes had gone back there eventually, but for his own part he had been 'all over', as he put it, and he knew the City well. It was a sense of adventure, more than any discontentment, or any particular desire to live in the country, which had brought him on this present jaunt.

Their talk as they moved along the deserted streets and alleyways was of great interest to Bushtail, but it did not distract either of them from the more important task of leaving messages by way of scent for those foxes who would follow. It was vital, too, for Rudyard, no matter how well he knew the City, to have good, strong markings to guide him on his way back to meet up with Redvers. Never in all his playtime and games of make-believe had Bushtail used the scent glands in his tail so consistently, and certainly not to such useful purpose.

They came then to an open space where there were many old rusting vehicles which the humans had abandoned. They made a meal of a few rats which they caught, and Ranter said it would be a good place to make another halt.

On this occasion, however, Herman disagreed, and was about to start on a long speech as to how well he knew the route, when Rudyard interrupted and said, ''Don't bovver about this lot. The way we're headin' we got a right old skinful of grub waitin' for us. You surely knows it, mate, if you reckons you knows the way we're goin'.'

'Yes, of course, I know it,' Herman said, 'but I didn't know that you did.'

'Course I knows. Told you before. Knows everyffink about this City. Been all over.'

'Are you sure we're talking about the same place?'

'I don't know what place you're talkin' about, mate, but I'm headin' for where the humans brings all the cattle an' sheep an' all them in to kill 'em, an' skin 'em, an' cut 'em all up an' all that.'

'Yes, that's the place,' Herman agreed somewhat grudgingly.

As they moved off, Bushtail and Rudyard, making sure they were unobserved by the others, rubbed the backs of their tails against a couple of the old rusting vehicles. The scent they left told any fox who was a stranger to the area not to be tempted to lie up there, but to press on to the good feeding ahead. Rudyard said that Redvers would be quite sure to read the message clearly, and he was equally sure that Redvers would find reliable foxes in each party to whom he could explain what was happening, and teach them how to read the messages in the scent correctly.

On the way they passed through a small park with a pond, and near this Bushtail pounced on an unsuspecting frog that made a juicy morsel. He was hungry and, for all the promise of a good meal to come, he did not believe in passing up the offerings of the moment. He licked his greasy chops and cast a glance up at the moon as it came out from behind the clouds. The weather was indeed being kind to them.

For a short distance they travelled next through an area more like that in which Bushtail had always lived, except that they had moved away at last from the great clattering machines and the bright lights. And then they came to the buildings where the cattle and the sheep were killed.

Only a few dim lights were burning, and there was no sign or sound of human presence. But there were a couple of foxes outside in the shadows of the yard where there was an abundance of meat which had been discarded by the humans. The foxes already there exchanged no greeting and said nothing, which troubled Bushtail not in the least. So hungry was he after their long trek, and so rich and plentiful were the pickings now before them, that he even gave a passing thought as to whether there was any point in going on to the country after all.

But there was no time to dwell on such pondering, for the local foxes had long since gone, and Herman passed the word along that it was time for them to be moving if they wanted to reach the security of their next resting place before daylight. The grey dawn was already breaking, and birds were pouring forth their morning song by the time Herman guided them to the overgrown gardens of some old, large houses, which looked as if they were deserted. They could hardly have found a better place to sleep off their weariness and the after effects of their recent surfeit of rich living. Give Herman credit for that anyway.

The sun came out later, and Bushtail slept more soundly than on the previous day. Rudyard was near him, and the yellow coloured vixen was not far away. Towards evening the foxes showed signs of stirring, and Rudyard asked Bushtail whether he knew the vixen. All that Bushtail knew about her was that she had been at that earlier meeting, and that she had not been backward about asking a question and generally making her presence felt.

'She ain't a bad sort,' Rudyard said.

'Do you know her, then?' Bushtail said

''Course I knows her. She's one of our lot. Look out for her at matin' time.' And Rudyard rolled his eyes and said, 'Unless I beats yer to it that is. It's all fair in love an' war, mate.'

'What's her name?' Bushtail asked.

'Tinks.'

'Funny name, isn't it?'

'Her family's a funny lot,' Rudyard said. 'Always had big ideas. Called her Tinkerbell. But who's goin' to waste time tryin' to say a name like that? Tinks we always calls her.'

'Does she know about using her scent to leave messages?'

''Course she does. Me an' old Redvers told her. We wasn't leavin' nuffink to chance, mate. Not wiv that Ranter an' his pal Herman.'

'Can we rely on her, d'you think?'

'Nah, you don't never want to trust no female, mate. Only time a vixen's any good is matin' time. An' then just when you ffinks you got it all made they'll stand for any fox what fancies 'em.'

'But you and Redvers trusted her?'

''Course we did, mate. We didn't have no choice. She was the only one wiv us from our lot. We wasn't sure about you. But you go along wiv her now, only watch yer back as they says.'

'You'll be setting off back now, I suppose?'

''Course I will. Old Redvers'll be waitin' for me wiv anuvver lot.'

'Do you know any of them?'

''Course I do. Ginette'll be there wiv her family.'

'Her family?'

'Her young uns. Six on 'em. Two on 'em like me an' Redvers, ffree on 'em more like Tinks an' her family, an' one on 'em nearly black, an' nobody seems to know where he come from.'

Rudyard held his nose to the breeze for a time, went over to say something to Ranter and Herman, and then moved quietly away in the gathering dusk. Bushtail soon found Tinks to be friendly enough, and it was not long before she said, 'Rudyard said you know all about leaving scent messages for him and Redvers.'

'And so do you,' he said.

'Yes, I know. And they're relying on the two of us from here on.'

After that they went on for some distance in silence, each marking certain posts or gateways with scent from time to time, and then Bushtail made so bold as to ask her whether she had any plans for mating next season.

35

'Don't be daft,' she said. 'That'll be for Comrade Ranter and the committee to decide.'

'Who said so?'

'It's in the constitution.'

'Maybe when we get into the country things'll be different.'

'Oh no. Ranter says that we'll change things to suit ourselves. We'll live as we've lived in the City and show the country foxes how much better our way of life is.'

Well, Bushtail said to himself, Rudyard had said never to trust a female, so he'd keep his thoughts to himself.

'Do you have any other ideas, then?' Tinks said.

'Not exactly,' said Bushtail. 'But I thought it was about time they let me have something better than I've had so far.'

'Maybe we can think about it,' she said.

'What, are you on the committee or something, then?'

'I have some small influence,' said Tinks. 'But we have to get there first.' Then she moved away to rub the back of her tail against the iron guard of a young tree growing on the corner of the pavement.

The moon had begun to wane and it was long before dawn when they found themselves amongst newer houses with large gardens and nice lawns. Herman said it was where the humans lived who went into the City every day, and they were still good to the foxes. It was nowhere near the big clattering machines and the bright lights, and the dreaded vans for taking the foxes away, and if they kept hidden by day it would be a good place to rest for the next day.

What Herman had said soon proved to be true when they found themselves in a large garden with decaying vegetables piled in a great heap in the corner. And here they found all manner of tasty slugs and beetles. But there was much better than that. There was another City fox there when they arrived, and when he saw them he moved away. He had been eating something at the edge of the lawn, and this turned out to be some very sweet-tasting pieces, shaped something like nuts, which the humans had put out.

All six foxes had started eating them when Ranter said, 'Don't look now, Comrades. The humans are watching us.'

Bushtail could not resist the temptation of a sly glance at the house, and there, sure enough, were two human faces framed in an upstairs window. The tasty morsels having

36

been cleared up, all six foxes knew exactly what to do. They drifted into the shadows of some great shrubs and waited. Their patience, born of long experience, was soon rewarded.

It was not long before a human came out with a large bag to sprinkle more of the sweet-tasting pieces on the lawn, and she could be seen to be putting something else out as well. No sooner had she returned to the house than the two faces were back at the same upstairs window, and then the faces of two children appeared at another window.

'Don't be too hasty, Comrades,' Herman said. 'This is all part of the game. We're not supposed to know we're being watched. Give 'em a chance to get excited because they won't be seeing us after tonight.'

When they eventually emerged from the shadows, the foxes found, not only a generous helping of the little pieces, but also some juicy bones with meat still on them. It was a good way to end the night's trek before the break of day, when they found some thick undergrowth near a large garden where they could sleep until the next night.

Night was drawing in when Ranter called them together to decide who should now return to the place of the big homes of the humans to meet up with Rudyard and the next group. Apart from Tinks and himself there were only two others from whom Ranter and Herman could choose. One was the other vixen, whose name turned out to be Nina, and Bushtail guessed that Ranter would not want to see her going back. That was no doubt why he sent the other one, a dog fox whose name Bushtail never discovered, but who looked as shifty a character as Bushtail had ever seen. Bushtail wondered whether they would ever see him again, because Tinks had told him that Nina knew this other fox, and she said he had lost his nerve and had already been talking about going back to the City. The whole undertaking could be wrecked if something like that happened.

It was a great comfort to Bushtail to think of the messages he and Tinks and Rudyard had been leaving so carefully in their scent all along the way.

Chapter 6

THE SCENE CHANGES

Reduced now to five in number, whilst they waited for the first news of those who were following and due to join them soon, Herman led them from the gardens to a lane where there were a few dim lights, but where all was quiet. And then they were in a field.

For the first time in his life, Bushtail was in a field. And he stood and listened to the silence, and he let the peace flow over him.

The moon had not yet risen, but there was a pale light from the stars and the faint glow of the lights of the City in the distance. Whatever the future might hold he was glad he had not succumbed to any such foolish ideas as had crossed his mind, however briefly, when they had been feeding so well back there at the place where the humans took their animals to kill them.

He wondered where Redvers and Rudyard were, and how they were faring, and he rubbed the back of his tail by the gate post. Now, more than ever, his instinct told him this was important. Nina had known something about that other fox sent back by Ranter and Herman. Maybe they were not quite as smart as they thought they were.

His thoughts were far away when Ranter cut in on them. 'Comrade Bushtail,' he said, 'why are you playing silly little games at such a time as this?'

So the great Ranter had seen what he was doing had he,

38

and imagined that he was still playing games. Yes, definitely not as smart as he thought he was.

A dreamy, faraway look stole over Bushtail's cunning features as he said, 'Well, you know, Comrade, it is so marvellous to think that you and the wise Herman have led us so far and so safely on this great adventure, and here we are in this wonderful new land you promised us that I am so very happy it makes me feel like a young playful cub again. Do you not feel the excitement, too, Comrades?'

'Yes, indeed Bushtail,' Herman said, visibly pleased at having had his wisdom praised, and at the same time having been thus associated with their great leader, Ranter. 'Yes, it has been a great responsibility and a great endeavour on our part, and it is gratifying that you should feel as you do. But we have far to go as yet, time is of the essence, and this is as nothing to the delights which await us out there.'

He cleared his throat and was evidently about to embark on one of his great speeches when Ranter said, 'We have no time to dwell on such matters now. Time, as you so rightly say, Brother Herman, is of the essence. Yes, indeed. Of the essence. But it is necessary that we convene a meeting with a view to making some small revision to our plans should that be considered advantageous until such time as we are joined by more of those who are following us.'

'With respect, Comrade,' said Bushtail, whose heart sank at the thought of such a prospect without Redvers or Rudyard for support, and by no means certain how much dependence he could place on Tinks, 'we are so few in number that we cannot expect to contribute much to the discussion. I am sure I speak for the two vixens as well when I say it is better to leave all in the care of you and Comrade Herman for the time being.'

'Well, Bushtail, I am glad to hear you say that. And if that is how you feel,' said Ranter, 'I am sure it speaks well for your judgement. Yes, indeed. It speaks well.'

Tinks and Nina did not demur, and Herman set off ahead of them across the field.

It was not long before they came to a road, and Herman said, 'This great road, Comrades, leads far into the countryside. We shall follow it, but we shall not use it. We shall follow it from this side of the hedges. Even so, it will provide us with some good living.'

Well, Bushtail had to admit to himself, whatever Herman's other shortcomings may be, he certainly knew the way he was leading them, for before long they came to a place where the humans pulled into the side of the great road in their cars, to walk about and talk their strange language, which Herman claimed to understand, and to eat some food and then leave some very nice scraps behind them. When the humans had gone, Herman led them through the hedge and they found a fair meal without having to hunt for it. Bushtail had heard vague stories of creatures called rabbits, which made good eating, but apparently the saying was, 'First, catch your rabbit.' Maybe they would learn about that another day.

There was even better to come, however, because a short distance further on, Herman led them to a place which was almost reminiscent of the City they had left behind them. There were buildings and lights everywhere, there were cars coming and going, and humans leaving scraps beyond belief. Truly, this was all it had been made out to be. It was growing late, and it was no trouble to steal about in the shadows, picking up scraps here and there to feed to their hearts' content. And here and there the humans sat in their cars, and threw scraps through the windows, and waited for the foxes to move in quickly to snatch them away and to take them into the shadows to eat them before coming back for more, and Bushtail began to think that perhaps the stories were true after all, and that the people in the countryside really were the friends of the foxes.

Soon after leaving this place, where Bushtail and Tinks both made sure to leave messages, they came to a village, and Herman had no trouble in leading them on a detour round it. It was just outside this village that they came to some small fields near one of the big dwellings of the humans. They were not unduly surprised to find two foxes there already. Big, strong foxes they were, dark in colour, and with distinct black crosses on their shoulders. They looked alike in most of their features, except that one had a white tip to his tail, whereas the other's was black.

Unlike the few strange foxes they had encountered on

their journey through the City, these foxes seemed friendly enough and made them welcome.

'You are country foxes, I suppose, Comrades,' Ranter said.

'Oh, aye,' one of them chuckled, 'we're country foxes all right. I can tell thee that for sure. But I don't know so much about this Comrade business. How about thee, mate?' he said, turning to his companion.

The second fox gave a sly grin and said, 'Ah, well, if it's Comrades it is, there's a job here we got our eye on. It's too much for us to tackle on our own, like. But there's enough of thee to help us, so like I said, if it's Comrades it is, then now's thy chance. There'd be some good feeding out of it. Where d'you come from, then? Not round here I'll warrant.'

'No, indeed,' Ranter grinned. 'Far from it. We're from the City. We're planning to settle down in the country.'

'Well look at that, now,' said the first fox. 'I thought I hadn't saw thee about before. Been here long?'

'No, indeed,' Ranter said, 'we're on our way now. Just passing through.'

'In that case,' said the country fox, 'we'll teach thee a few country tricks now to start with.'

Ranter exchanged an amused look with Herman, as much as to say there was no harm in humouring these characters. Just as if they could teach the City foxes anything. Bushtail noticed the look which passed between them and knew full well what they were thinking. For his own part he thought it was very friendly of these two country foxes to be so helpful.

He was not nearly so prepared, however, for the violence that was to come.

The idea, said the one with the white tip to his tail, was to make a real killing. In the next small field was a pony belonging to the child of the humans living in that dwelling, and this pony had recently given birth to a foal. They had tried to attack the foal, but the pony had fought them off. So what they wanted was for two foxes to annoy and distract the pony whilst the rest of them tackled the foal.

'We can manage that between us,' said Whitetip, 'if the vixens'll pester the pony. They ought to be able to do a bit of a job like that. Just keep her busy and on the move.'

Thus it was that Bushtail was initiated into something of

41

the killing instincts of his ancestors that had lain dormant for generations since time out of mind.

True, he had occasionally killed rats and mice, frogs and beetles, and small birds in their nests, and eaten their eggs. But, for the most part, his life had been one of living on the plentiful scraps left by the humans. He had never thought much about his people as having been killers. But now he knew.

Tinks and Nina moved off to do their bidding with a will, and the two country foxes went for the foal with a savagery such as Bushtail had never known. As the helpless young creature, without its mother's protection, was cornered, one of them sprang to snap at its throat and the other followed. It took few such vicious snaps to rent and tear, and to bring the foal to the ground. The end came quickly and, as Bushtail tasted the hot blood on his lips, he felt that primaeval lust to kill, and the two country foxes and Ranter and Herman tore and ripped into the tender stomach, what time the five of them were joined by the two vixens, whilst the pony whinnied, and stamped her hooves in a circle all round them.

For a full hour they gorged themselves, until the whinnying of the pony disturbed the humans, for lights came on in their dwelling, and voices were heard.

'That's it, then,' said Whitetip, 'time for us to move. Hope you boys had a good time.'

'Splendid, thank you,' Ranter said. 'Most entertaining. Haven't eaten so well for ages. You live near here, I suppose?'

Whitetip grinned. 'Don't thee believe it, boy. I'll tell thee one thing now and that's not two. If thee'rt going to live in the country, don't thee ever make the mistake of shitting on thy own doorstep. We've got a long way to go, and we're off.' And, with that parting word of country wisdom freely offered, they melted into the darkness.

The voices of the humans were now close at hand, and instinct was enough to tell Ranter and his following to delay their departure no longer. Listening from a safe distance they could hear the voices of the humans grow louder, and they did not need Herman to tell them they were voices raised in anger and distress.

Herman resumed his duties as guide, but they had not

travelled far before they came upon a small field where there were two goats. The foxes were not hungry, but the urge to kill was now strong within them, even though they had little need to eat. It seemed to be all part of the fun of country living. Nor were the two goats the full extent of their slaughtering for the night, for they found a little hutch with some white rabbits in it, and it was no trouble to break in there and kill them, too.

It was still some time before first light when Herman led them to a sequestered place where a stream flowed fresh and clear, and here they drank and cleansed themselves of the blood on them before they settled to sleep for the day. For the second night since setting out they had gorged themselves, and they slept well. Yet Bushtail had disturbing dreams and misgivings. Sometimes as he dozed he heard again the voice of that country fox and wondered what his parting advice had meant. Bushtail still trusted nobody, but the two country foxes had been so friendly that he believed they had meant well with what they had said.

All along the way Bushtail had left messages in his scent for Redvers and Rudyard to know as far as possible what had been happening. And now he knew he must go back himself.

For one more night, however, they remained in the good place to which they had come. They had, as Herman said, eaten their fill, which should last them for some time, and there would be plenty of grubs and small creatures on which they could feed if they wished, so now they could take their rest and consider future plans. But Ranter and Herman agreed that it was Bushtail who would now have to go back, whilst they and the two vixens waited for some of the others to join them. They had found a good place to wait.

It was during the second night that Bushtail and Tinks foraged together, and Tinks said that Nina was not happy.

'She thought that all that killing was a bit daft,' Tinks said.

'Maybe so,' Bushtail said. 'Didn't she enjoy herself?'

'She enjoyed herself all right, but she's been worrying about what that country fox said.'

'What about it?'

'She couldn't make any sense out of it. But Comrade Ranter said not to take any notice. The two of them had been good fun, he said, but they were only a pair of poor country fools after all was said and done.'

'Maybe so,' Bushtail said again. If Tinks was talking things over with Ranter he was going to keep his own misgivings to himself. With the four of them left on their own there was no knowing what plans they might be making. Even so, he still had to put some trust in Tinks.

'Have you told any of the others about us leaving the messages?' he asked, as casually as he could.

'D'you think I'm daft?' she said.

'I just wondered.'

'Well, keep wondering, then. I'll tell that pair as much as it suits me to and no more.'

'Good,' Bushtail said. 'I'm glad to hear that. But you'll keep leaving the scent messages for me, won't you?'

'Leave them for you?' Tinks looked puzzled. 'How d'you mean, leave them for you?'

'Well, when you go on from here,' Bushtail said.

'We're not going on from here. Not that I've heard anyway.'

She seemed to be telling the truth, Bushtail thought. So, if they were planning anything, they hadn't let on to the vixens. And that was what Rudyard had said, watch your back, and don't ever trust the females. It was in their nature anyway to suspect everybody, even though he was as convinced as ever that Ranter and Herman wanted as many City foxes as possible to reach their great new settlement in the country.

From now on he would be on his own. At least he would have the time to think things over quietly to himself.

Chapter 7

A WORRYING TIME

For the first time in his life, Bushtail was truly on his own. Always in the City other foxes had been within call. They had lived in community and, over many years, had developed new customs and a new way of life, as the likes of Ranter and Herman never ceased to remind them. Perhaps, when they reached the country for which they were heading and settled down at last, they might be able to do something about this wretched constitution about which they heard so much. More than once recently there had been signs of its being called into question.

But they hadn't reached the country yet, and here he was, not only on his own, but in strange surroundings, and his heart was heavy. Yes, the killing had been good, and so had the food, but it had all been done through their joint effort together. None of them would be able to kill like that by themselves. Even those strong country foxes had needed their help. That was one of the benefits of their community life. But he still puzzled about what the country fox had meant by what he had said as they were leaving. And, according to Tinks, Nina was worried, too.

The killing had been a great experience, far more exciting than anything he had ever known or could have imagined. And what a variety of good, fresh food there was. So far, everything had given them good reason to believe that the rosy picture painted by Herman was true, and maybe even better than he had been able to say.

45

He was unhappy about his feelings towards Herman. At the outset, when this great move in their lives had first been talked about, he had extolled Herman's virtues, and been impressed by the experience and knowledge he claimed to have of the countryside. But he had been rude to old Redvers and had derided what now seemed to have been his wisdom. Yet, in spite of Herman's apparent familiarity with the route they were taking, Bushtail had seen much in him which, to Bushtail, suggested that he was suspect. Earlier in life he had listened to him because he was his father, but now he was coming more and more to rely on his own judgement. And, in his own judgement, he had seen enough to change his opinions about Redvers and to know that he was nobody's fool. It was Redvers who had sent Rudyard along, and that in itself said much for Redvers' wisdom. How glad he would be to meet up again with either of them, and how terrible it would be if their venture were to fail now after they had been permitted this glimpse and taste of what was yet to come. A pity he had such misgivings about that fox they had sent back after Rudyard had gone. Bushtail had a nasty feeling about that one.

Yes, on his own, he had plenty of time to think, and his thoughts were not always such as to set his mind at rest.

He paused awhile and held his nose to the breeze. The smell of the country was good. There had been the scent of flowers and of things growing in some of the parks and the gardens of the City, but it had not been the same as this. In the City there had not somehow been the same freshness. Nor, in the City, where there was for ever light in the sky, was there such wonderful silence as here. Then, from somewhere nearby, there came the screech of an owl and, from even closer, it was followed almost immediately by the slight sound of movement in the bushes, and a handsome animal, much about his own size, came out in front of him. Grey he was, with a white stripe down his face. Bushtail prepared to run, but the animal looked at him carefully, grunted, turned and went on his way. From all the stories Bushtail had ever heard of the countryside he knew this must be a badger. Harmless creatures by all accounts, and many good stories had been told of some of the things the foxes had done and the badgers had been left to take the blame. Well, if they were as stupid as that, they had it coming to them. And then all was silent again. The moon had not yet risen, and the weather was still dry. A shower or two of rain might not come amiss, to freshen things and to make the soil moist and easier for nosing out the grubs and beetles. And then, in the midst of all his wandering thoughts, he stopped, with every nerve alert. No sound had there been, but he knew danger. He was upwind, and it was difficult to know what had troubled him. More than once he had picked up the scents which he and Tinks had left, but this was different, and some instinct told him to leave the route by which he had been returning so carefully.

Cautiously, one foot raised, his big ears forward, he stood, and then, with infinite care, he circled slowly until he was downwind and, with his wet nose poised, waited until the smell came to him. And when it came, it was the smell of death.

A long time he stood there. He had known from his own scents as he retraced his footsteps that he was near the place where they had carried out the marvellous killings, and fed so well, and had then killed some more for the sheer exhilarating delight of it all. But this smell was different.

The smell of death on those creatures they had killed had been rich and satisfying. But not this. For this smell of death was the smell of foxes, and Bushtail knew real terror. There was the smell of humans, too, and it was not a good smell. Whatever Herman had said about the humans in the countryside, where no man's hand would be against them, there was something wrong here. There was anger here, and death. It was a place of real and terrifying danger, and he longed to be away from it.

But he did not panic. Cautiously he withdrew, even more cautiously than he had approached. And then, with his heart almost bursting with joy and a great relief, at the trunk of a tree he picked up the familiar scent of Rudyard. And the message, which was clear to read, said come back to the place of the dwellings where the humans had put food out for them.

All along the way he picked up the scent of the places he and Tinks had marked, but he was miserable with foreboding, wondering what had happened, and what might yet lie ahead. But, whatever had happened at that place of death,

47

at least it seemed that Rudyard was alive, and that thought raised his spirits. He was almost happy by the time he came upon a pheasant's nest with the pheasant sitting on her eggs. Had he had his wits about him, he could have had the pheasant. He would know better another time. As it was, he pounced too late, but he scoffed her dozen eggs, and it gave him new heart. He had learned long ago by the big ponds in the parks of the City how to deal with the eggs in a nest, by biting off the top of each egg and licking it clean inside, but he hardly thought that birds in the country would be daft enough to make a nest on the ground. Perhaps they were as daft as Herman had said the country foxes were.

But dawn was creeping over the horizon, and he needs must break his journey. That day he found a quiet place to rest and, on the second night, he came to where Rudyard was waiting for him with eight other foxes.

It was a sorry tale that Rudyard had to tell, and it came as no surprise to Bushtail to learn that the fox they had sent back as a guide had deserted the cause. Rudyard had seen nothing of him, but word had come from Redvers that he had arrived back with his own community and had said he had changed his mind and intended to stay in the City.

'There was bad blood there, mate,' Rudyard said. 'We knew his lot all along. But we knew as you an' Tinks would be leavin' us some messages, so me an' Redvers talked it over like, an' he said to give it a go, an' that's what I done.'

Ten of them there had been, including Ginette and four of her cubs. They were growing up now and feeling independent, and her other two cubs had said they were staying in the City.

Well, Rudyard said, they had found the places where Bushtail and Tinks had left the scent messages, and it had worked like a dream, with no trouble at all. They had all eaten well at the place where the humans took their animals to kill them, and had then followed easily to the gardens where the humans put food out for them. It had all seemed too good to be true. And it was.

Rudyard found it difficult to go on with his story for a time, but then he said that, after leaving the gardens where the humans had fed them, they had reached a terrible place, and Bushtail knew it was where they had met the two country foxes, and he told Rudyard of everything that had happened there.

'Well, that's it, mate,' Rudyard said, 'the humans was waitin' for us.'

One of Ginette's cubs, apparently, had gone on a little way ahead and picked up a nice piece of meat which the humans had put out for them, and the next anybody knew he was stretched out in agony. A couple of them went to see what was the matter with him, only to find that his brother's foot was gripped by some terrible steel thing with sharp pointed teeth, and he was tugging at it and trying to bite through his own leg, but he couldn't do anything. So they knew there was something wrong and they tried to get away from there, but almost before anybody knew what was happening, a couple of them had wire round their necks and were pulling for all they were worth but all to no avail.

'So that's how it was,' Rudyard said, 'an' I said as it was best to turn back an' see what was happenin', an' that's when I left my message for you, an' I ain't half glad to see you an' all, mate.'

'Not half as glad as I am to see you,' said Bushtail. Then he turned everything over in his mind and said, 'Tell me, something, Rudyard. Why do you say the humans were waiting for you?'

''Course they was, mate. Stands to reason, don't it? After what you lot done, they was goin' to get their own back.'

'But how would they know you'd be coming?'

'Nah, they wouldn't know 'twould be us. They'd ffink the same lot might be comin' back again.'

'That's it, then,' said Bushtail. 'That explains it.'

'Wot explains wot, mate?'

'As they were leaving, one of the country foxes said he'd give us a good tip for living in the country. He said never shit on your own doorstep.'

'Well, that's wot you done. Same as that lot wot I told you about broke into where all them turkeys was. So we've learnt sumffink for anuvver day.'

Apart from himself, he said, only Ginette and one dog fox had managed to return, but now they had been joined by six more, and they had lived in hope of having some word from Bushtail before deciding on their next move.

49

Not least of Rudyard's worries was that one of the foxes to have joined them was none other than the notorious Arter, a close associate of Ranter's, a member of Ranter's committee, and strong for the constitution. Those there were who thought that Arter might succeed Ranter one day.

'If you've never seen him, mate, you ain't missed nuffink,' Rudyard said. 'He got one of them old long snouts, an' he looks sly even for a fox.'

Rudyard and Bushtail did not let him in on their quiet discussion, as a result of which Rudyard set off back for the City to meet and consult with old Redvers. They had agreed that if they were going to have any more defectors, or any more such losses at the hands of the humans, then maybe it would be no bad plan if they could be joined by some more foxes and to travel with a greater number. It was not the way they had planned things originally, but circumstances altered cases.

Soon after Rudyard left, Arter appeared on the scene, and Bushtail saw that Rudyard had not been exaggerating when he had said he looked sly. And he certainly had a longer than usual nose. He was, like Ranter, of the ordinary yellowish brown colour, and his long snout, as Rudyard had so disparagingly referred to it, was about all that distinguished him from a score of others. Immediately, he convened a meeting, but Bushtail said he could not attend because he had travelled a long way, there had been much to distress him, he was tired, and he needed a good rest.

'I think, Brother,' Arter said, 'Comrade Ranter will take a poor view of this when it is reported to him. You are in a position to give us vital information to enable the committee to decide on our next move. The committee, therefore, require your presence.'

Bushtail's travels had already taught him a thing or two, and his experiences since leaving the City had begun to build up his self-confidence. It was going to take more than the long-snouted Arter to intimidate him.

'Isn't there something in the constitution about it?' Bushtail said.

'What d'you mean, the constitution?'

'Don't tell me you haven't heard of the constitution.'

'What does the constitution have to do with it?' Arter demanded to know.

'Everything. There's a special provision as it applies to our community which refers to such a contingency. Point of order. You don't have a committee as things stand at the moment.'

'I must warn you, Brother, that the constitution applies to all foxes in the City, whatsoever, wheresoever and whensoever, without let or hindrance, and without exception absolutely. Comrade Ranter will confirm this when this most unfortunate matter is reported to him.'

'Ah, well,' said Bushtail, 'that's it, isn't it. You'll have to find your way to Ranter first of all. And without me to guide you, you won't ever get that far. And I'm not setting off until I've talked to Rudyard. And that won't be until he's talked to Redvers.'

'Where is Comrade Rudyard now?'

'Ah, well, that's it again then,' said Bushtail. 'If I told you, you'd know as much as I do. Now you run away and hold your meeting, tell 'em Comrade Ranter said it's a key issue if you like, and I'll find a nice quiet corner to sleep it off.'

'I demand to know in the name of the constitution,' Arter snarled, 'where is Brother Rudyard?'

'He's talking to the great, and the good, and the most truly wise Redvers.'

'And where is this Redvers character?'

'Redvers?' said Bushtail. 'Why, he's talking to Rudyard, of course. Where else would he be, and what else would he be doing, when Rudyard has gone off in order to find him and to talk to him?'

Bushtail curled his bushy tail round his nose, put one ear forward and one back, and settled down to sleep with an idea in his mind that he had not made a new friend.

Chapter 8

A CHANGE OF PLAN

For a week the foxes remained near the place where the humans put food out for them, and each night the humans appeared at the windows to watch them.

It was easy living, and Bushtail came to know Ginette and the other fox who had managed to find his way back with her and Rudyard from that awful place of death. His name was Rusty. The two of them talked to Bushtail of their experiences during that time, but they told him little he did not know, and he kept his own counsel. On one thing the three of them were agreed. However attractive country living may be, they had come to know too much of the dangers for themselves at first-hand to be rushed by this Arter character into moving one step further until Rudyard returned with word from Redvers.

The name of Redvers was still respected by many. Fixed in his opinions though he was known to be, and by no means in favour of this move to the country, he had nevertheless been sufficiently big-hearted to put himself at the service of those who did want to go. Not only was he known for his great wisdom, but he was also known as never having been a wholehearted supporter of the constitution. More than one fox had a regard for him if only because of that, so it was a great delight to others, as well as to Bushtail, to find when Rudyard returned at last that he had brought Redvers with him.

Just as dawn was breaking they arrived, as the first birds were beginning to greet the day with their morning song, and four more foxes came with them. Arter immediately called a meeting.

'Point of order, Comrade,' said Rudyard. 'Can't meet in daylight. It's in the constitution.'

The four new foxes were clearly highly amused.

'In the constitution?' Arter said.

''Course it is. This new lot. They got to be swore in. Ain't you never heard about that, or don't you know nuffink?'

'This is most irregular,' Arter spluttered.

'Then you ought to take sumffink for it,' said Rudyard, again to the great delight of the newcomers, and the strong suspicion grew in Bushtail's mind that no doubt these characters had been carefully selected, either by Rudyard or Redvers or, even more likely still, by both of them together. And Bushtail was more than happy on that score, however much this foolery and light-hearted disdain might be to the annoyance of Comrade Arter and his like-minded mates.

It was time now for sleep but, first of all, Bushtail wished to have a word or two with the only two foxes he felt he could trust. And, for their part, Redvers and Rudyard had many questions to ask of Bushtail, and were anxious to discuss certain matters with him. He had, after all, been close to everything that had happened along the way, and seen at first-hand how everything had been done to cause the tragedy when the humans had waited for them, to poison them, and to set such terrible traps to catch them and kill them.

The three of them knew enough to understand that their safety, and the safety of all the others, would depend on more care than had been taken so far. Whatever might happen about the constitution when they had all reached the country and settled down, this was no time to be arguing about it. All that could wait until another day.

When they had found a secluded corner far back in the thick growth, Redvers said that the four foxes he and Rudyard had brought with them were anything but well disposed towards Ranter and the constitution. All of them had ever been such characters who would prefer to go their own way. Like Rudyard, they were not all that keen on the idea of settling in the country, but they were more than ready to join in the adventure, even if they came back to the City later. To them, it was all good fun. If they happened to annoy Comrade Ranter and any of his confederates, so much the better.

When night came, Redvers would be setting off back to the City to collect the remainder of those foxes who would be waiting for him, and he would probably have to move them in two groups. They agreed between themselves that Rudyard should now travel on with Bushtail and the rest. Redvers said he knew he could rely on Rudyard and Bushtail to leave good scent messages, and they should be able to rely on any of the four new foxes to come back at various stages along the way to help to guide them forward. Ivan, Redvers said, would see to that. It seemed that he was the moving spirit amongst the four, and certainly more confidence could be placed in any one of them than in the cowardly fool Ranter had sent back and who had failed them so badly. To Bushtail, it was evident that they would owe a great deal to the wisdom of old Redvers if their venture were ever to result in success.

Their plans had been well laid by the time the lights of the humans were coming on and night was drawing in, which was the signal for Arter to call them together for a meeting. He had scarcely had time to launch into his opening preamble, however, before Rudyard interrupted.

'Point of order,' he said.

'What do you mean, point of order?' Arter snapped.

'Point of order. Message from the great Ranter and the great Herman. You tell him, mate,' Rudyard said, and turned towards where Bushtail was sitting on his haunches, his tail wrapped comfortably round himself, and looking very pleased with life.

'Is this true, Comrade?' Arter demanded to know.

''Course it's true,' said Rudyard.

'Then why not let him speak for himself?'' Arter was clearly becoming rattled.

'That's it then. How can he give his message wiv you gabbin' on like you was the only one as knowed anyffink. An' if you was to ask me you don't know nuffink. But this here Bushtail, he been out into the country, like, ain't he? Stands to reason, don't it? He was wiv Ranter wasn't he? Stands to reason he'd have a message, don't it?'

The four foxes were enjoying this exchange thoroughly, whilst some of the others were looking somewhat ill at ease.

'Well, then, Comrade,' Arter said, addressing Bushtail, 'what is this message from our leaders?'

54

'Very simple message,' said Bushtail. 'Very simple indeed. Time is of the essence. Those were their very words. Herman spoke them first, and Ranter agreed. Of the essence. As spoken by Herman, and agreed upon wholeheartedly by Ranter. Of the essence.'

'So what does that mean?'

'What does it mean? It means that time is of the essence. So cut the gab as Brother Rudyard calls it, and no meetings.'

'This is all most unusual,' Arter said. 'I must demand of you to know, what were Comrade Ranter's exact words?'

'His exact words? I'll tell you. The great Ranter said, ''We have far to go as yet, time is of the essence, and this is as nothing to the delights which await us out there. We have no time to dwell on such matters now. Time, as you so rightly say, Brother Herman, is of the essence. Yes, indeed. Of the essence.'' That's what he said, and that's what he meant, so it's time for us to be making a move.'

'But we have not yet sworn in our four new Comrades,' Arter protested.

'Too late now,' Ivan said. 'We have no mandate from our local committee as yet. Point of order. Have to report back to them first. And there's no time for that. What was that message the great Ranter sent? Time is of the essence. That's it. Of the essence.'

'Hear, hear,' his three mates chorused.

'I fear you do not seem to be taking this matter as seriously as the grave situation would appear to warrant,' Arter said.

'Nah,' Rudyard said, with a sly wink at the four adventurers. 'We ain't wantin' to talk about no graves, mate. We wants to stay out o' them.'

'Hear, hear,' Ivan's three mates chorused again.

'Point of order,' said Redvers. 'That's enough of this bickering. We all have far to go in our different directions, and the nights are getting shorter. Those I have left behind in the City will be anxious to have word of what is happening. One day, if all goes according to plan, we shall meet up in the country. Until that time it will be necessary for Brothers Rudyard and Bushtail to assume full control.'

'What do you mean, full control?' Arter snapped. 'They are not even on the committee.'

'Nothing to do with it, my friend. They have already had experience of the route that is being taken and of some of the

55

dangers involved. And no doubt Rusty and Ginette will be able to offer some good advice as well, because they, too, have travelled part of the way and have seen overmuch of the hazards.'

Ginette seemed more than pleased to have been thus noticed, but the fact that Redvers should have dared to suggest that they should even contemplate consulting a mere vixen was too much for Arter.

'You seem to forget yourself, Comrade,' he snapped again, in even worse temper. 'Most assuredly Comrade Ranter will hear of this.'

'Point of order,' said Rudyard. 'State of emergency.'

'Exactly,' Redvers said. 'Standing Orders suspended.'

Arter made as if to speak, but Redvers had already begun to move away quietly into the night, and all that was to be seen of him was the distinctive white tip to his tail with its even more distinctive fine black ring round it.

As they prepared to move away, in another attempt to reach their final destination out in the country, Bushtail realised how well Redvers, no doubt in collusion with Rudyard, had planned things. Whatever might happen about their precious constitution when they all met up again far away from the City, there should not be too much danger of this inexperienced bigoted fool, Arter, leading them into more trouble.

Apart from himself and Rudyard, Bushtail reckoned they could bank on the support of Rusty and Ginette. It had been a tactful move on the part of old Redvers to mention them as being of some importance in their deliberations, and it was plain to see where Ivan and his three mates stood. Whatever allegiance any of the others might or might not feel they owed towards Comrade Arter, they would no doubt have enough sense to see the wisdom of what was now being done.

Yes, Redvers was serving the cause very well. It would be even more to the good of the cause if, when they eventually reached the country, he could be persuaded to settle there rather than return to the City.

Chapter 9

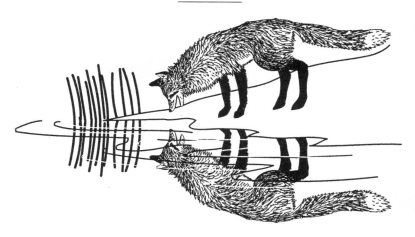

THE JOURNEY RESUMED

Having set off at last, Arter seemed to have accepted with as good a grace as possible the fact that, not only had he been outsmarted, but that he had lost face in the eyes of those foxes who had come with him and who could have been expected to heed his every word. Did he not have the authority of the committee behind him?

Bushtail chuckled to himself. Yes, Arter had all the authority of the committee behind him, but most of the members of that committee were scattered far and wide, and many changes might well have taken place by the time they were all able to meet up again. Bushtail had no illusions as to Arter's true feelings, but there was still a long, long way to go before he would be in any position to show his teeth. And Bushtail was only too conscious of the fact that on himself and Rudyard, and maybe a few of the others, would rest the great responsibility of seeing them safely through to their final destination.

The first part of the way was familiar to Bushtail, and he did not think they need fear any great danger as yet as he led them from the place of the gardens to the lane where the few dim lights were, but where all was quiet.

As soon as they had reached the field, he rubbed the back of his tail by the gatepost, just as he had done the last time he had come this way, and he had noticed Rudyard doing the same thing as they had come along the lane. But not only did they leave their messages for Redvers. They also picked up their own scent which they had left as they had returned from that first disastrous part of the journey.

Then they reached the road, and Bushtail said, 'This great road, Comrades, according to Herman, leads far into the countryside. He said we shall not use it, but we shall follow it from this side of the hedges. Even so, it will provide us with some good living.'

They came then without undue incident to the place where the humans pulled into the side of the great road in their cars, to walk about and to eat some food, and then leave some nice scraps behind them. When the humans had gone, Bushtail led them through the hedge and, once again, there was a fair meal without having to hunt for it. Then he led them to the place which was reminiscent of the City, with the buildings and lights everywhere, where the cars were coming and going, and the humans were leaving scraps beyond belief.

The City foxes agreed it was all it had been made out to be as they stole about in the shadows, picking up food here and there to feed to their hearts' content. And, in some of the darker places away from the lights, the humans sat in their cars and threw scraps through the windows. Then they waited for the foxes to move in quickly to snatch them away and to take them into the shadows to eat them, before coming back for more, and Bushtail told the others how, on that previous occasion, he had begun to think that perhaps the stories were true after all, and that the people in the countryside really were the friends of the foxes.

This line of talk was too much for Arter, however, who said, 'I cannot accept your thinking, Comrade. It is not politically correct. If Comrade Herman said that the great road leads direct into the country, then we may rest assured that it does so. Yes indeed. We may rest assured. But what I find disturbing is the incorrectness of your thinking. Indeed. Most disturbing. How can you possibly doubt the assurances of Comrades Ranter and Herman that the reports are true that the humans in the countryside are our friends?

We cannot discuss these matters now, but I must give you fair warning that what you have said will have to be the subject of a full report to the committee when so much else concerning recent devious thinking and behaviour will be under discussion.'

'Wot you bovverin' about now, mate?' Rudyard said.

Arter gave him a vicious look. 'Have I not made myself clear, Comrade? I am greatly disturbed by the attitude of some of the Comrades. It is not in line with the thinking of the committee who have to safeguard the constitution and ensure correct thinking at all times.'

'That's it then, mate. We better ffink more proper from now on, an' I'll have a word wiv this here Bushtail an' sort him out, like. I been ffinkin', mate. That Redvers character got it all wrong. Now we're out in the fields, like, it's only right for one of the committee to start leadin' us again. Stands to reason, don't it?'

'Hear, hear,' said Ivan and his three mates in chorus.

Rudyard gave Bushtail a knowing wink, and Bushtail understood that Rudyard was alive to the danger.

Easily flattered, Arter said, 'I find your change of attitude most encouraging, Comrade. It speaks well for your judgement. Yes, indeed. It speaks well.'

Bushtail smiled to himself. He had heard similar words from Ranter, when he himself had been playing for time. And he reckoned he could make a fair guess as to what Rudyard had in mind. He was sure of it when Rudyard said, 'Wot you wants to do now is go on a bit ahead an' we'll follow close behind. We're on the right paff.'

Arter made as if to break into a speech, but Bushtail said, 'With respect, Comrade. Let us still not forget the message of Comrades Ranter and Herman. Time is of the essence. The way is clear. We follow this line of hedges until dawn.'

'Very well,' said Arter, 'I shall lead on.' And, with a couple of quick flicks of his tail, on he went ahead of them.

They had gone but a little distance when Bushtail stopped, licked his nose to make it moist, and held it up to the wind. He had remembered the smell of steel from that place of death, and he said to Rudyard, 'This is it. You recognise it?'

''Course I do,' Rudyard said.

The other foxes had all stopped and were looking at Rudyard and Bushtail.

After several minutes of silence, Rudyard said, 'If you lot got any sense you stays wiv us. If you ain't got no sense, you follows him. If he reckons Herman is that smart after all the trouble wot him an' that Ranter landed everybody in, then he got it all comin' to him. But I tell you sumffink. I reckons he won't be comin' back an' we won't see him again. So now we can keep goin' in peace an' work out wot it's best to do wivvout no constitution.'

He waited a few moments. No fox spoke or moved, and Rudyard said, 'Right then. It's up to me an' Bushtail to work it out togevver wiv a bit of help from Rusty an Ginette maybe, an' we follows Bushtail because he been furvver than any of us.'

Still nobody spoke. Then Bushtail raised his nose to the breeze and, moving on quietly to sniff at a wooden post, set off on a wide detour of the place of death.

They had travelled slowly and, with the utmost caution, until they came to a small copse which Bushtail thought might be a suitable resting place if they were not able to reach before daylight the place where he had parted from Ranter and the others. Rain had fallen the previous day and, on the moist air, scent carried well. Feeling that the place of the greatest danger had been passed, he had just settled down to discuss their position with Rudyard when, out of the night, there came to them the smell of a strange fox. Yet Bushtail recognised it. Sure enough, within minutes, one of the two country foxes of their earlier meeting came to join them. This was the one with the white tip to his tail.

Truth to tell, the country foxes had led them into such madness that they had caused terrible trouble for those who had been following them, but Bushtail recognised that much of the trouble had come from their own City ignorance of country matters. And he had a warm regard for this Whitetip, because it was he who had so readily given him the good advice. He had been nothing if not friendly, and so he proved again now.

The story he had to tell them was not a happy one. He knew all about the slaughter of the second lot of foxes from the City, and eventually had met up with Ranter and the other three foxes with him. He had told them what had happened, and so Ranter had decided that the venture had

60

met with failure, and that they might as well go on by themselves.

'A pretty little vixen that was with 'em,' he said. 'I wouldnt have minded having a go at her myself come next winter. What was it they called her? Tinks, or something, wasnt it?'

'So they've gone, have they?' said Bushtail.

'Oh, aye, they be gone for all. I tell thee that for sure. They said as how they be going to set up somewhere one of 'em knows. Herman or something they called'n. Said they was going to teach the country foxes how they lived in the City, and start up a new constitution. Do thee know anything about this constitution business then?'

'Yes, we knows about the constitution,' said Rudyard.

'Good thing is it?' Whitetip grinned.

'Why d'you ask, mate?'

'Because if they ever gets as far as they be reckoning to go, that's where old Reynard lives. He'll give 'em constitution. Aye, constitution. He'll learn 'em a thing or two about constitution for all.'

'Well,' Bushtail said, 'If they've gone from where I left them we might as well stay here until tomorrow night and talk things over.'

'No, don't thee stop here,' Whitetip said. 'Twouldn't be safe after that outing we had together that night. Too close. Come thee with me and I'll show thee a good place between here and the wood thee'rt making for with that nice stream. It'll be safe there for thee for a spell.'

It was, as Whitetip had promised, a good place to which he brought them, and he was good enough to stay with them all day. When night came he led them to the wooded area where Bushtail had left Ranter, Herman, Tinks and Nina.

It was, as Bushtail had remembered it, a good place, with the clear stream, shady fern, and green and grassy glades where they could sleep in the sun by day. But no sign was there anywhere to be found of Ranter or the others. Maybe Ranter had not planned for any of them to go off on their own, as Redvers had all along feared he might but, when the first moment of crisis had come, that was what he had done.

It came as a relief to Bushtail to find that, whatever their great leaders may have had to say about the country foxes and their stupidity, there was no question about their being

61

helpful, especially if they were anything like Whitetip. He had given them vital news, had shown them to a safe resting place, and now had brought them here to this place which they had been seeking. But, as Bushtail said ruefully, much good it looked like doing them. For their great leaders had gone, and they would have to work out what they were going to do. Tempting though it was to think of a settlement where they were, there were those who now looked to him and Rudyard to lead them all the way, and certainly there were those coming on with Redvers who would expect no less. Such had been the way of their society, living in community, for as long as anybody could remember.

Even in this, Whitetip was a great help. Although it was far, far away from his own territory, he said, he knew of the area to which Herman had intended trying to lead them, and it was said to be a good place. But, the way they were planning to go, it was not going to be easy to reach . He said he had offered to tell them a much better way to follow, but the ones they called Ranter and Herman had said that they knew the way. The two vixens, however, had protested that it would be far more sensible to be guided by him, and so he had gone with them for the first part of the journey. And here Bushtail saw a ray of hope, because there was still the chance that Tinks would have left some messages along the way.

Their best plan, Whitetip said, would be to follow the stream for only a short distance and cross it just before it joined the big river. If they failed to do this, the river would be difficult to cross later on, and there were smaller rivers, and many large villages and towns where the humans lived, all of which would require long journeys to avoid.

The way he told them to go had something else in its favour. It led much more through fields and open country and, now that the rain had come, the grass and the corn and the hedgerows were growing well, so there was plenty of cover for them if they wished to travel sometimes by day.

It was shortly after midnight when Whitetip left them, and once again before leaving them he offered them some good advice. But this time he did not speak in riddles they could not understand. He simply told them not to play in the growing corn and the long grass, because it would draw attention to their own presence, it would make the humans angry and, if there were other foxes following from the City, the humans would probably be waiting for them.

'It's not quite the same as shitting on thy own doorstep,' he said, 'but thee finishes up with the same smell, and the same thing'll happen to thee as last time if them humans turns nasty. They be bad enough in the first place for all, without thee going and making 'em worse.'

Bushtail was sorry to see Whitetip go, but he was grateful for what he had learned from him, and he had certainly made it clear that he did not share Herman's ideas about the humans being such good friends to the foxes. Right at the start old Redvers had voiced his misgivings and doubts about what Herman had been trying to tell them on that score. The time had come when they would have to work out their plans for the future.

There was no moon now, but it was a pleasant night. Occasionally an owl screeched as it hunted along the distant hedgerows, but their own immediate concern was not for food. Whitetip had been kind enough to give them some ideas as to how and where they could look for food in the country, since they would no longer be able to rely on the dustbins and rubbish tips of the City. Their first consideration was to decide who should return to meet Redvers and the next two groups and, almost without discussing it, they knew the answer. It would have to be Ivan and one of his mates.

'Do they know about leaving messages?' Bushtail said.

''Course they do,' said Rudyard. 'D'you ffink old Redvers would have let 'em go wivvout teachin' 'em? Stands to reason, don't it. They been leavin' 'em all the way.'

Bushtail had to admit that he hadn't noticed and that he still had much to learn.

Chapter 10

MORE TROUBLE

With time to spare, Bushtail explored the area where they had rested, sniffing here and there in the hope that he might pick up some sort of message from Tinks. He did not allow himself to become too optimistic because, judging by what Whitetip had told them, it must have been some time since Rudyard and the others had departed. He had enough sense to expect any scent that had been left to be faint by now.

Every now and again he picked up the scent with a news item from some country fox or other, but he did not understand such messages completely. Even so, it was yet one more proof that these country foxes were not so stupid after all, and maybe far better organised than Bushtail or Ranter had realised. He understood a couple of these messages to be referring to the fact that the City foxes were passing through and what their plans seemed to be. Then he discovered a post with several different scents on it, and it seemed to contain all sorts of messages, so that Bushtail concluded it must be some sort of accepted place for passing on information of importance to the country foxes. He found it all very interesting and enlightening.

It was coming near to daylight, and he had just about lost hope of coming across any scent left by Tinks, when he detected it, so distinct was it, on a large stone near the edge of the woodland area. As he had anticipated, it was only faint, but it was unmistakable. It clearly told him what they had already learned from Whitetip, that Ranter had been in a panic and ordered them to move on, but it also confirmed that they were taking the route which Whitetip had recommended to them. And that was a real relief, because there would be every chance that Tinks would have left other scent markings further on. It meant, too, that her messages could be understood and seemed to be reliable.

For three more nights they stayed in this pleasant place, but an awareness had come to them of the truth of Whitetip's warning that there was now no immediate and easy source of food, with none of the easy pickings of the City dustbins and gardens, and no humans putting out food for them. The occasional beetle or worm was acceptable and welcome, but by no means sufficient to sustain them.

Although Whitetip, in his usual helpful way, had given them some useful hints on finding their own food, there were still twelve of them, even though Ivan and another had gone back to meet some of the others. Nor could Whitetip, however well-meaning, teach them overnight the arts and tricks of their country ancestors, which they had long since forgotten, of how to scent and stalk and kill, or even to find the best and easiest places from which to steal. And it was not made any easier when some of the birds went on ahead, calling and flapping their wings in alarm to warn of their approach.

There were other creatures about, too, with whom they were in competition for such food as was available. And these stoats and weasels, buzzards and owls, and even the badgers, all of whom had been identified for them by Whitetip, were greatly experienced in supplying the needs of their own existence.

Nor was that all. Added to their inexperience in these new surroundings and conditions, was this realisation of what was now evidently an embarrassment of numbers. Earlier on their journey, in the light of the dangers with which they had been faced, they had discussed it and taken what had seemed to be the sensible decision to travel in greater numbers from here on. It had seemed sensible, because it would mean there would always be a fox or two to spare to go back to guide others, and always some over in case of any untoward happening. Now it was beginning to look as if it had not been such a good idea after all. As they moved ever further into unfamiliar surroundings, they began to understand that one fox could move with stealth, and remain concealed for long periods, where such a crowd as they were could not. The wise old Redvers had warned of such a difficulty long ago at that meeting when the possibility of a move to the country had first been discussed.

It had seemed to be a great benefit, on the night of that killing and feasting, to have the strength of numbers which made it possible. Which was one more example, according to Ranter and Herman, of the wonderful advantages of living in community. Yet, from what Whitetip had said, from what they had seen for themselves, and from what Bushtail and Rudyard were beginning to understand from the news items which the country foxes were constantly leaving for each other, they kept very much to themselves, each to his or her own territory. Apparently they lived alone, and for much of the time hunted alone. Nor did it need the brains of a City fox to work it out for himself that one fox could find enough food on which to live where a dozen would find it more than difficult. Unless, of course, they used their strength of numbers to kill as they had killed that time before. But they remembered only too well what the terrible outcome of that had been.

'I'll tell you sumffink, mate,' Rudyard said, when they had considered their predicament from every possible angle. 'That Herman knowed wot it was like an' he knowed he couldn't manage on his own. An' I ffinks as he persuaded everybody wot a wonderful idea it all was, an' I ffinks as he don't know nuffink. But I'll stick wiv it now an see wot some of these country vixens got to offer a bit later on.'

'I thought you fancied Tinks,' Bushtail said.

''Course I fancies Tinks. Every old dog fox I ever seen fancies Tinks. But you takes your chances where you finds 'em, mate.'

'And what about the constitution and selection by committee?'

Rudyard gave Bushtail a sly and knowing look. 'Wait till we gets to where Ranter an' the rest of 'em is an' I'll tell him sumffink about constitution. But we ain't there yet, mate. An' if we goes on messin' about round here we ain't never goin' to get there.'

And so, on the fourth night they set off again. As they went they found good places to stay overnight and, as Whitetip had said, everything in the country was growing, so they travelled sometimes for short periods by daylight. But, for the most part, it was by night that they found such food as they could, and learned how to catch and kill, a rabbit here and there, and occasionally, the young of the ground birds when they came upon their nests. Bushtail recognised them from his previous close encounter with the hen pheasant, which had given him that good feed of eggs. But it was slow going, and several nights would sometimes have to be spent in one place to give them a chance to find enough food before starting off once more.

One thought that comforted and sustained them, however, was the fact that Tinks had left her messages along the way and, faint though the scents were, they were sufficient for Bushtail to know they were still pressing on in the right direction. Then, when everything seemed to be going well, there came the ominous scent of a warning. And the message was such that Bushtail and Rudyard fancied that something had happened here, the same as had happened once before on that fateful night with Whitetip and the other country fox. Bushtail moistened his nose, held it to the breeze, and smelt steel. It was a smell that meant death, and it was becoming all too familiar to him for his peace of mind. The other foxes had stopped, too, to follow Bushtail's movements, and then he spoke quietly to Rudyard.

They retraced their steps for a short way to a small area of dense woodland, and there, every sense alerted to any possible danger, they stayed all that night.

Quietly, and with the utmost caution, as dawn was breaking, Bushtail and Rudyard moved forward again to a place where there were little wooden huts scattered all over a field, where many of these beautiful pheasant birds roamed freely with their young.

But there, by a gap in the hedge, was the message in the scent which Tinks had left. Faint though it was, it told them clearly enough that Ranter had decided to go in for a good killing, as they had done on that night with the two country foxes. But the scent of humans and the steel nearby was much fresher.

Rudyard and Bushtail already knew that Tinks had heard from Whitetip what had happened to the other foxes at the place of the great killing. Ranter and Herman, too, had been told the same story. Yet they would seem to have gone in here for more easy killing knowing full well what the deadly consequences would probably be for those who were following them.

It was a matter of much concern which Rudyard and Bushtail had to put before the rest of them.

'You can carry straight on if you likes, mates,' said Rudyard. 'But I ffinks that if you do you'll be the same as that Arter an' you won't be comin' back. If you got any sense you'll still stay wiv us. Wiv the old firm. Me an' Bushtail.'

Rusty and Ginette had seen enough for themselves when they had survived the first disaster. No doubt they had told the other City foxes of that experience, and in any case there was nobody left in their party at present to talk about committees and the constitution. They may not have known much about the ways of the country when they set off from the City, but it needed little experience for them to recognise that this was a matter of survival. There could be no constitution or way of life more important than that.

It was not a happy thought for either Bushtail or Rudyard to realise how Ranter had been prepared to betray them, but they had to admit that it was their nature. Bushtail had himself said to Redvers never to trust anybody, and it was Rudyard who had said especially never to trust a female. Even so, without Tinks they would have lost track of the others long before this.

There was only one thing to be done now, and that was for one of Ivan's mates to go back to lead the others as far as this and to warn them of the peril. He could do no more, but would have to wait here with them in the hope that Bushtail and Rudyard could somehow or other find a safe way round this new place of danger and hope to pick up scent from Tinks once more. Then one of them would have to come back here to collect them. To this extent, at any rate, it was useful to have a sufficiency of numbers.

That same night, whilst they were yet undecided as to their next move, or even in which direction they should be travelling, they had a visitor. A rather ordinary sort of country fox he seemed to be, but it soon became clear that he was fully aware of their predicament.

'I heard about thee,' he said. 'Bit off more than thee can chew is it Charley?'

'What d'you know about us, mate?' Rudyard said.

'Ho, ho,' the newcomer chuckled. ''Tis mate now is it? Last time I heard tell, 'twas Comrades. But don't thee fash thyself on that score, my old foxy chal. I heard from Whitetip as thee calls'n how thee was shaping.'

'Have you seen Whitetip?' said Bushtail.

'Don't need to see'n. Left a message. Said as thee might need a bit of help.'

'That's kind of you,' Bushtail offered.

'No skin off my nose. Them flash coves as was here haven't learnt nothing. Wasn't satisfied to take one or two. Had to go wading in and kill for all they was worth. Now the humans is out with their steel traps and wires and we all got to keep clear.'

'Would you happen to know which way the others have gone?'

'Aye, aye. I knows all right. Whitetip set 'em on the right road for all, and that little vixen was leaving her messages a proper masterpiece. Got the hang of it straight off. A sharp little piece by all account. Old Whitetip took a proper fancy to her. Don't thee be surprised to see'n turning up come clicketting time. Unless he meets up with something better. But a couple of 'em I've heard tell of reckons they wouldn't mind a bit of fresh from the City.'

'Maybe some of these country vixens ain't so bad if it come to that,' Rudyard said.

'Aye, but they reckons a change is as good as a rest for all. Th'only trouble is there always seems to be twice as many of us as there is of the vixens, so it's every fox for hisself. Thee might be lucky and thee might not.'

'Ah well,' Bushtail said, 'we've a long way to go before we come to that. So can you tell us where we ought to be making for now?'

'Aye, aye I can tell thee that for all. But keep thee well clear of where the pheasants is for the next few nights' travelling.'

The way was not difficult, but it took them in a wide sweep from the route they should have been taking, until they came to the place where the corn was growing.

A good place it was, and some of them stayed in the cool shade of the growing corn long after daybreak. That was a danger of which the country fox had not thought to warn them, but for a long time afterwards Bushtail would tremble at the thought of how close they could all have come to disaster. As it was, it had meant the death of Rusty, who had been with him and two of the City foxes. One of them was a member of Ranter's committee.

Bushtail thought they had seen and heard the last of the great clattering machines when they left the City behind them, but now, hard though it was to believe or understand such a thing, there was a great clattering machine in the field. Worse than that, as it went round and round, it also kept coming nearer and nearer. As the day wore on and the hot sun rose in the sky above them, so the four foxes retreated towards the centre of the field, only for the great clattering machine to keep bearing down upon them, until at last there was no place to turn and the humans were shouting. So the four of them dashed for the safety of the woods and Rusty was the first to go. Then it was that there was the roar and flash of fire from the gun, and Rusty tumbled over and lay dead as the others redoubled their efforts in sheer terror. There was another bang as they raced over the rows of cut straw. Bushtail saw one of the two City foxes check momentarily, but he recovered and kept going.

As soon as darkness fell they moved on, and it was relief beyond measure to Bushtail when, before dawn, he came again upon the scent which Tinks had left for them.

Chapter 11

DESTINATION

As Bushtail reflected on all that had happened he felt almost ashamed of himself to think how he had scoffed at old Redvers at that first meeting, and how he had quoted Herman as saying that the humans had to keep their guns locked up and that it was possible to be well away before they could use them. Well, they had used one sure enough on poor old Rusty, who had survived that first disaster, only to die in such an unnecessary way. Was there not, indeed, so much to learn about this country living? They had already learned more than enough about Herman's much vaunted knowledge of the countryside. The way things were going it was beginning to look as if their wonderful constitution could be dead and buried before they ever had time to settle in the country.

One thing was for sure, he said to Rudyard. They would have to stay where they were for a time and send the last of Ivan's mates back to warn the others of this new danger. How lucky it was that Redvers had sent them along and had instructed them in the leaving of messages by means of their long-forgotten scent glands.

'That wasn't no luck, mate,' Rudyard said. 'Old Redvers is dead crafty. Knows a ffing or two I can tell yer. Had that Ranter weighed up long ago. If anybody can see the rest of 'em ffro safe it'll be him.'

'Funny thing, really,' Bushtail said. 'He wasn't a bit in favour of the whole business in the first place. But if we ever succeed it'll be more because of him than that Ranter and his committee and all the rest of 'em put together.'

'I tell you one ffing, mate. If you're still reckonin' to stay in the country you better try an' persuade old Redvers to stay on wiv you.'

''I'm hoping he will. And what about you? Will you stay?'

'I've told you before, mate. Let's see wot some of the local talent's like first. But we ain't there yet. And now we got to stay here till we see wevver some of Ivan's lot can get ffro.'

Yet another moon had come and gone, and now once again a great yellow moon was riding high in a clear sky. The time of year had come when the nights were lengthening and had begun to grow colder. It would have been good weather for travelling, but they had to wait. Then the City fox that had seemed to have escaped the shooting was seen to be sick and in pain. He had nasty sores breaking out on his side where the shot had hit him. As he grew steadily worse, the sores began to smell, and at last he dragged himself away into the bushes to die. It did not trouble Bushtail as much as it might have done, for that fox had kept quiet and said nothing about being a member of Ranter's committee. He had more than enough to worry him without concerning himself unduly about the fate of any of Ranters' allies.

Thus far, when Bushtail had felt despondent along the way and wondered whether there was any hope of carrying on or whether to turn back, something had happened to give new heart. But never had anything revived his drooping spirits like the arrival, in the early hours of the following morning, of none other than old Redvers himself in the company of the irrepressible Ivan.

'You've done very well, young Bushtail,' Redvers said.

'Not so young these days, my old friend,' said Bushtail. 'This business has made an old fox of me.'

'Put it all down to experience. 'Tis a great teacher. And it'll serve you in good stead when you reach that place for which you're heading.'

'I'm not so sure I want to go there now I've seen as much as I've seen so far. I'm beginning to think that maybe Ranter and Herman didn't know as much as they thought they did.'

'All the more reason for you to go through with your original plan. You've learned so much more than they have as you've followed after them and paid the price for their mistakes. I hear they've caused great trouble by their foolishness and their ignorance of the countryside.'

'How much have you heard, Redvers?'

'I fancy Ivan's told me as much as he knew. But you seem to have had more trouble again since he left you. At the place where the pheasant birds were. You did well to avoid trouble there.'

'You heard about that, did you?'

Old Redvers was clearly amused. 'Oh, yes. I heard about that all right. From that gipsy sort of character. Never told us his name. But evidently acquainted with that Whitetip who seems to have been taking such an interest in you all. There's not much these country foxes don't seem to know about what's going on. And they seem to be very friendly and helpful, too. The idea seems to be that one or two of them have designs on our Tinks.'

'They can forget that,' said Rudyard. 'They ain't the only ones wiv an eye to business there.'

Redvers looked more serious, and said, 'But you had worse trouble, I believe, where the corn was growing.'

'You've been told about that as well, have you?' Bushtail said.

'Not told. Picked up a few news items the country foxes had left on their postings. They leave their scent messages very effectively. Something we shall need to study more carefully.'

So Bushtail told him of what had happened there, and how they had lost Rusty and the member of Ranter's committee.

'Not a good type that one, I'm afraid,' Redvers said. 'He could have caused much trouble later on. Like that dreadful Arter. According to what Ivan tells me Rudyard was too smart for him. But I don't suppose you've heard about what happened to him.'

'We can only guess,' said Bushtail.

'Oh, I can tell you for sure. We met him on his way limping back to the City. Apparently his foot had been caught in the sharp teeth of one of those terrible steel traps, and in desperation he'd managed to bite through his leg before the humans came, and he was heading back for the City on three legs. Didn't want to talk much about it. But Whitetip told us the rest. Whitetip had met him and assured him he wouldn't last five minutes in the countryside once the humans came out on their horses and with their great dogs.'

'Course he wouldn't,' Rudyard said. 'If he was as daft as he was on four legs he wouldn't last long wiv one of 'em missin. Even wiv the constitution. Stands to reason, don't it. 'Twas like stealin' milk from a blind kitten dealin' wiv him.'

Old Redvers mapped out the next moves carefully. He had come back to his original thinking and recognised the dangers and the difficulties when too many of them travelled together. In any case, he said, it looked as though the worst of their troubles could be over, so the plan now was for him and Ivan to go back to organise the safe passage of the others. Meanwhile, Bushtail, Rudyard and the rest should go on to the next suitable place of shelter, hoping they could pick up some further messages from Tinks on the way, and wait for them there.

It had lifted the hearts of Bushtail and the others to have had this meeting, and all the more so because it had been so unexpected, and at a time when their spirits had been so low. Even as they had watched the distinctive dark ring on the white tip of Redvers' tail disappear into the moonlight they had felt uplifted, because there went with it the promise of better times ahead. At this juncture, however, their previous good fortune deserted them. Faint though the scent left by Tinks had been for some time, it had nevertheless been there, and had served its purpose well. Bushtail did not believe she could have failed them now, but nowhere, try how he would, could he pick up her scent anywhere. Nor did Rudyard, going off in different directions, meet with any success either. The delays along the way, as they had fallen further and further behind, had meant inevitably that the scent had weakened and now was lost.

For two nights they travelled, leaving their own scent for Redvers to follow, until they came to a wooded bank where they decided to stay to await events. If the worst came to the worst, at least they could hope to be joined eventually by Redvers once again. But they calculated that it could not be for several nights yet.

And then, before they had worked out any plans as to what it would be best to do if Redvers did not arrive, they had another surprise. However unexpected it had been when Redvers and Ivan had turned up a few nights ago, it was as nothing compared with their astonishment when a familiar scent came to them on the breeze and, minutes later, Tinks trotted into the clearing, where the moonlight dappled the grass with the shadows of the leaves on the stunted trees.

It was an amusing story that she had to tell. For their part they saw no point in telling her how much had happened after Ranter had decided to move on, or how such news had come to them. Neither Rudyard nor Bushtail thought it would be good to impart such knowledge as she might pass on to Ranter. Let him learn things the hard way for himself. And it soon became clear to them that the vixen had been sent back by Ranter to suit his own ends, and for a definite purpose. Somewhat to their surprise, that purpose was to lead them all the way to where Comrades Ranter and Herman had set up their headquarters. They had reached their destination, and Tinks was to lead them to the great ones.

Apparently, when Ranter had learned from Whitetip of the trail of disaster the leaders had left in their wake, he had decided to abandon to their fate all those who were following, saying they would have to fend for themselves. He was, by that time, much taken with the idea that Herman had mentioned at their original discussions as to how it would not be good tactics for too many of them to arrive together. So Ranter now thought that the four of them should move on immediately to the great wood, which Herman knew so well, and set up home there.

'We met a few country foxes at different times during those early days,' said Tinks, 'and I must say they seemed friendly enough. Comrade Ranter immediately started to explain to them about the constitution, and how our way of life could work to their great benefit. They seemed to be interested and listened to all he had to say and, of course, Comrade Herman supported him by explaining that he had himself been brought up in the country and therefore knew all about it as well as about the advantages of living as we had lived in the City.'

'And how did they take that?' Bushtail asked.

'They didn't seem all that interested, so Ranter decided to call a meeting.'

75

'And what happened then?'

'Nothing.'

'Wot d'you mean, nuffink?' said Rudyard.

'Nobody came.'

Following that, Tinks told them, Ranter tried twice again, but still nobody turned up.

'And then,' she said, 'another fox turned up.'

She paused at this point, and then said, 'Quite the most magnificent specimen you ever could see.'

'My goodness, Tinks,' said Bushtail, 'you seem to be impressed. Don't tell me his name is Reynard?'

'Yes, it is. But how would you know that?'

'As I once said to the lately departed Comrade Arter, if I told you, you'd know as much as I do.'

'What d'you mean, lately departed? Where's Comrade Arter now?'

'Gorn,' Rudyard said. 'Back to the City.'

'Why would he do a thing like that?'

'Met wiv a most 'orrible accident, that's wot he done. A most 'orrible accident, gory an' 'orrible. Lost a leg, that's wot he done.'

'Did you do it to him?'

'Nah. 'Course not. Done it to hisself.'

'What d'you mean, done it to himself?'

'Chewed it off, that's what he done. 'Cos he's stupid. That's why he done it. An' that uvver little creep wot that Ranter put in to report everyffink to him wivvout tellin' us. He went an' got hisself shot. Dragged hisself off into the bushes an' died a most 'orrible death, that's wot he done.'

'But Comrade Ranter knows nothing about all this.'

'Nah. 'Course he don't. Stands to reason, don't it. He's stupid, ain't he?'

'Well, I can tell you now, he'll be mad over this. He was mad enough when those stupid country foxes failed to come to the meetings he'd convened.'

'But you haven't told us about this Reynard character yet,' Bushtail said.

'There's nothing to tell. Except that he told Ranter he was wasting his time.'

'And what did the great Ranter have to say about that?'

'That's when he got mad and said we'll see about that. Then, when Reynard had gone, Comrades Ranter and

Herman talked it over and said if the country foxes wouldn't see sense we'd fall back on the first plan and move in our whole community. It looks to me as if they realise we can't manage on our own without the other City foxes. So that's why I'm here. He sent me to find you if I could.'

'Good job you left your scent along the way for us,' Bushtail said.

'You done a good job there,' Rudyard added.

'Always pleased to oblige,' said Tinks.

'Let's hope you'll be as obliging when it comes mating time,' Bushtail said.

'I've told you before, that's up to the committee.'

'Don't believe everyffink you hear,' Rudyard said. 'You might find that ffings is changin' when we meets up wiv Ranter.'

'That sounds interesting. Nina seems to have taken more than a passing interest in the handsome Reynard.'

'And some of these country foxes have taken more than a passing interest in you, too.'

'We'll think about that when the time comes.'

'From what I've seen of some of these country foxes,' said Bushtail, 'you mightn't have much time to think about it.'

'You make it sound exciting,' Tinks said. 'But isn't it time for us to be going?'

'No hurry,' Rudyard said. 'Some of our comrades here is tired an' hungry. They needs some sleep an' to go an' look for some food. Until then Ranter can sweat a bit.'

For five more days and nights they waited, until Ivan arrived to say that Redvers and a whole host of others were on their way, and then they allowed Tinks to lead them on to their destination, what time Rudyard and Bushtail made sure that they left copious scent markings as they went.

Two nights travelling was all it took them to reach the edge of the great wood to which Herman had led them, and there Ranter asked for an account of their journey. Rudyard was pleased to oblige, telling him no more than it suited him to tell. He was more than pleased to say that the trusted Arter had defected, but gave no account of his accident 'most gory an' 'orrible'. Tinks could do that if she wished.

Bushtail weighed in with the information that Ranter's trusted undercover committee member also was no longer with them, and it left them still short of numbers. When they had set off the last time from the outskirts of the City there had been fourteen of them. Apart from Ranter's two, they had lost Rusty, whilst Ivan's quartet had all returned at various stages and had not rejoined them as yet. So that left only Rudyard and Bushtail, along with Ginette and four others who now looked so hungry and forlorn that even Ranter must have had poor hope of forming a committee at this stage. They certainly did not look like committee potential.

'Well, Comrades,' he said, 'I cannot pretend this is anything other than most disappointing. Indeed, most disappointing. We must therefore call a meeting forthwith, even inviting any country foxes who may care to come, and see immediately about giving our constitution effect as of now.'

'Nah,' Rudyard said, 'we ain't talkin' about no constitution. We're waitin' for Redvers. He's the one wiv all the brains. If it hadn't been for old Redvers, none of us would ha' been here, not after you'd done a daylight flit. Maybe you was ffinkin' we didn't know nuffink about that. But we knowed wot you was up to, as soon as we heard about the flash coves from our old foxy chal. Me an' Redvers an' my mate Bushtail here. We ain't takin' no more notice of you, mate.'

Clearly affronted, Ranter said, 'You are not quite yourself after your long journey, Comrade. We shall therefore ignore that uncalled for outburst. There will be loyal and experienced committee members travelling with Comrade Redvers and, I feel sure, advising him. When they arrive there will be a full and frank discussion on all the key issues, and the committee will deal with these matters in the proper manner in compliance with our tried and trusted constitution.'

'Listen, mate. There ain't no committee here, an' there ain't no meetin'. We'll see wot Redvers got to say about it when he comes. An' until he comes, mate, you can go an' piss up yer leg an' play wiv the steam.'

And with this telling, if not highly erudite, remark, Rudyard wandered off into the bushes.

78

Chapter 12

REYNARD OFFERS ADVICE

A handsome fox indeed was Reynard, bright golden russet of coat, with a dark mask and strikingly white underparts. No exaggeration had there been when Tinks had told them of him. In size, too, he was above the average, with a magnificent brush, shading to a black-tipped tail, completing the description which Tinks had not given them in detail.

Whitetip had given them fair warning, so that Bushtail and Rudyard, at any rate, had some idea of what to expect. They greeted him with respect, therefore, and a show of some friendship, when he came to where they were resting the night after they arrived.

Ranter and Herman, however, had received no such intimation of his existence, let alone his reputation, and, in any case, were rather more full of their own importance, whereas Reynard was polite and friendly.

'I trust thou has settled in comfortably,' he said.

'Indeed, thank you, Brother,' said Ranter. 'Yes indeed. So far it is all we had been led to expect. And we shall be pleased to help you all we can, of course.'

'So I understand,' Reynard said. 'I hear thou hast been putting forward some rather unusual ideas. It has been told to me.'

'Unusual to you, maybe, my friend, but not to us. You see, we are far advanced in the City, and we come to you to show you how our way of life can be of great help to you in improving your own standard of living.'

'Thou really thinks thy City ways are much better then?'

'Oh, yes. Let there be no doubt whatsoever. No indeed. No doubt whatsoever. I do not hesitate to say it has been a great disappointment to us that your people have not been more forthcoming in availing themselves of the opportunity to meet with us and to hear of all that we have to offer. Indeed, on three separate and specific occasions, I personally convened meetings to afford your people the opportunity to learn of so much which would be to their great advantage. It is a sad reflection on their attitude to life that on all three occasions nobody turned up. A sad reflection indeed. I repeat. A sad reflection. Sad indeed.'

'Thou must understand,' Reynard said, 'out here in the country we're not much given to meetings.'

At his most horrified and indignant, Ranter said, 'It is the way we have always managed things in the City.'

'Well,' said Reynard, 'I'm not just sure that thy City ways would be quite right for us.'

'Oh, my dear sir, you must not think we come to you without knowing all about the country. No indeed. Comrade Herman here has a very great knowledge of it. In fact, he was brought up in the country. In his early days he lived amongst the humans and even came to understand their language.'

'Point of order,' interpolated Rudyard. 'That Herman knows nuffink, an' this Ranter knows nuffink. An' me an' Bushtail had word of you, Mister Reynard, from Whitetip an' that foxy chal, an' we'll be chuffed to bits for any advice you can give us. An' so will our mate Redvers. He ain't here yet, but he's on his way, an' he's the one wiv a lot of brains.'

Reynard gave them a knowing look, and said, 'Yes, my friends, I've had word of thee, too. Thou hast served a hard apprenticeship on thy way here. It'll serve thee in good stead. And I've also heard tell of thy Mister Redvers. I'm told he's very civil and very wise. I don't want to sow dissent amongst you, but I'm looking forward to meeting him. We all have to live, and I hope we can live at peace. When Mister Redvers arrives I'll come back with two good friends of mine, Blinker and Trotwood, both very experienced in the affairs of life, and perhaps we can discuss these matters to our mutual advantage.'

Whereupon, leaving Ranter and Herman at a loss for

80

words and in ill temper, Reynard departed with disconcerting dignity.

Hungry after their long journey, Bushtail and Rudyard went in search of food. There were still many blackberries to make a nice tit-bit for a change, and then they came upon an orchard with a profusion of juicy apples fallen into the long grass beneath the trees, all of which was so much more satisfactory than having to hunt and kill. On one occasion, on the bank of the stream, they discovered a fine fish, which looked as if it had been caught by an otter and left, with only a piece out of the back of the neck having been eaten. The remainder made a most acceptable meal.

For two nights and days, Bushtail and Rudyard explored the woodland and the countryside together. There was much shelter, useful dens beneath the trunks of trees, there was thick undergrowth, and there were banks of fern near a stream that ran swift and clear. They avoided Ranter and Herman, and saw little of the vixens or of the other foxes. It was early on the third night that Redvers arrived with Ivan and one of his mates.

Scarcely had there been time to greet them before Reynard came into the clearing with two other foxes, and it was assumed that this would be the Trotwood and Blinker of whom Reynard had already spoken. Of the ordinary yellowish brown colour they were, with no particularly distinctive markings, but there was about them a bright-eyed alertness and general air of well-being, which Bushtail had never seen in a City fox. Blinker, as it turned out, had little to say, but blinked rather shortsightedly, what time he nodded his head wisely in approval as Reynard made the attitude of the country foxes clear. Bushtail thought he had been well-named.

Reynard came straight to the point and said that, if they wished to survive in the country, they would have a better chance if they lived on their own and kept apart, each to his own territory. Too many of them together would attract too much attention from the humans, with disastrous consequences. That, he said, would be asking for trouble and a certain way of being killed.

'Allow me, my friend,' Ranter interrupted, 'we have some considerable knowledge of this subject. We have lived in large communities for many generations in close proximity to the humans, and it is only fair to say we have found them most accommodating. Indeed, I would go so far as to say they are most kind. Yes, indeed. Most kind.'

'Quite so,' Herman added. 'And if I may be permitted a further observation as a result of my knowledge of the humans' language, let me say that there are great changes afoot. Yes, indeed. Great changes. There is indeed a groundswell of opinion, and more and more humans are saying that on no account must we be molested in any way. Perhaps you have not been made aware of this.'

'No, we hadn't noticed it,' said Reynard.

'Well, of course,' Ranter said, 'it is part of our purpose here to make you aware of these trends.'

'And do thee think that as well, Mister Redvers?'

Redvers had said nothing so far but, thus addressed, he cleared his throat and said, 'Indeed, I make no claim to any great knowledge of country matters. It's no secret, mind you, that I don't share many of the opinions of Ranter and Herman. But I come from a family with a long tradition of handing down stories through many generations, and I must admit I've heard little to make me think we're very popular with the humans of the countryside.'

'It's good to hear thee say it. Never forget one thing. In this land the humans is our only enemy. We can kill anything we fancies, as long as we can manage it, and feed off anything. But there's nothing kills us or feeds off us. And the humans don't like it when we takes their chickens or kills their lambs or small pigs or anything else we can get a hold of. They'll stand for so much, but no more.'

'You speak with authority,' said Redvers. 'As I say, I have no great first-hand knowledge of country matters myself, but what you say doesn't surprise me.'

'And all these foxes coming with thee? How do they feel about it?' Reynard asked.

'You know about those, do you?'

'Indeed we do. There's not much goes on around here as we don't know about. I'm told there be more than thirty foxes due in here as soon as they have the word from thee.'

'You never said a truer word, Comrade,' Ranter said. 'And amongst them will be sufficient members of the committee to have our constitution established and given effect before the mating season.'

82

Still completely unruffled, Reynard said, 'That makes it sound more interesting. We've heard a bit about thy constitution, so maybe we ought to hear thee tell us about it now to see what we can make of it.'

To receive such an invitation was more than Ranter could have dreamed of, and he launched forthwith into an impassioned exposition of the system which had led him to a position of such power in the community. And now the foxes of the countryside had the same wonderful opportunities being presented to them. Reynard and Trotwood and Blinker listened attentively, and seemed particularly impressed by the wonderful breeding plans for keeping the strain pure, and the foxes strong and healthy.

When he had finished, Reynard said, 'So what do we have to do to get our names on this list for selective mating?'

'It is good to find you showing some interest at last,' Ranter said. 'All you need do is adopt our constitution and you will soon be most enthusiastic. Indeed, I repeat. Most enthusiastic. With the mating season close upon us, you really should waste no time. I shall convene a meeting for you and ensure that everything is established on the approved lines according to our own standing orders.'

Reynard, Trotwood and Blinker exchanged satisfied looks. Reynard said they would be in touch, winked at Redvers, and then moved quietly away into the darkness with his two companions.

There was no moon these nights, and the weather had turned cold and wet. Whilst Ivan and the other fox went back to bring more than thirty foxes, including three families of growing cubs, on the final stage to their new home in the country, Redvers, Bushtail and Rudyard left scent messages for Reynard to say they would appreciate a meeting with him on their own, and it was not long before they received an answer.

It was the most pleasant interlude Bushtail had experienced since leaving the City. Not only was he in the company of two foxes who shared his opinion of the power-crazed Ranter and the scheming Herman, but he found this more recent acquaintance to be a refreshingly interesting and entertaining companion. Bushtail was glad he had come into the country, but it was for reasons which he recognised

83

as being rather different from those which had prompted him to advocate the move in the first place.

As Reynard began to understand their attitude, so he became more expansive and told them many stories of his own experiences, and of tales that had been handed down. Some of his stories concerned particularly cunning foxes that had been in these parts many generations ago and, like Redvers, were not only of his rich, red colouring, but had the same white-tipped tail with the distinctive dark ring.

In turn, he was interested to hear of the stories that had been handed down to Redvers from the long, long ago, and the pair of them had soon established a sound relationship. The drift of their talk then led on to show that Reynard and many of his associates were more than ready to be helpful in giving advice and useful information, whilst at the same time making it clear that they would do nothing to their own detriment. It was the law of the wild, and it was every fox for himself.

He went on then to admit that, to the country foxes, Ranter's talk of a constitution, and committees, and mating schedules was one huge joke. They had no intention whatsoever of attending any of his stupid meetings. He and Trotwood and Blinker had gone along to make them feel welcome and to try to help. If the fools did not wish to be told, then on their own heads be it.

'I doubt,' said Reynard, 'whether they'll last beyond the second winter.'

They were fortunate, he said, that they had not arrived a few weeks earlier in the year. Soon after the corn had been harvested, a few of the humans had been out on their horses and with their young dogs in search of the fox cubs. It was all part of the way the humans taught their young dogs to hunt, and it gave the vixens a chance to teach their cubs, who were now having to go out on their own in life, how to survive. The young ones from the City would have been slaughtered. Since they had been hunting the cubs, Reynard said, the humans had not been round that way on their horses and with the older hounds in any great numbers, but they certainly would be later on.

'And then,' he chuckled, 'we'll see how the Comrades gets on with their constitution for all. Aye, constitution! Some of them hounds'll give 'em constitution.'

One thing he wanted to impress on them in the name of friendship was that the country foxes liked their privacy, each keeping to his own clearly defined area. They resented intruders. At the same time, they used certain well-established posting places to leave many news items which were helpful and of interest to foxes over a wide area. That was why he had known of their advent long in advance of their arrival, and there was little he did not know of the great killing and the slaughter of the pheasants, with all the terrible consequences, as well as the confrontation with the humans where the corn was being cut. And, with a sly wink, he told them that the advance news included the general interest in Tinks, as well as Nina and Ginette.

It took Redvers and his two younger companions little discussion to decide that they wanted no further part of the Ranter and Herman nonsense, and Reynard said that he and Trotwood and Blinker would be more than happy to show them something of the area, and to tell them of some useful earths, where they could live the satisfying life of the country fox. For their own part some of them had already moved away from their old dens in the area where Ranter and company had decided to settle, in the certain knowledge that to live anywhere near them would be fraught with danger.

Redvers and his two friends, Reynard said, could set up quarters close to each other and leave messages for such times as when there was a carcass somewhere on which many of them could feed together, just as they could leave news of many other happenings of mutual interest. It was a good thing, he said, that they had practised this use of their scent glands to such good purpose on their journey from the City, for they would know all that was going on over a wide area of the countryside. It was clear that Ranter and Herman would be severely handicapped because of their lack of such knowledge.

'But Tinks knows,' Bushtail said.

'Ah, yes, Tinks,' Reynard said. 'But Tinks is a vixen, and she'll use her messages to suit herself. Bank thee on that. If she never let on to 'em along the way, she won't be letting on now for all.'

As they were about to part, Reynard said to Redvers,

'According to all I've heard, thee'rt not too sure whether to stay with us or go back to the City.'

'You seem to be remarkably well-informed,' Redvers said.

'Well, as I've told thee, news travels. Especially in the country. So hast thee decided yet?'

'I haven't had time to think about it.'

'Well, don't think too much. We don't want too many like that Ranter's crowd trying to take over here. I've listened to thy talk, and thee'rt one of us. Redvers,' he said, 'come home. This is the place for thee. Come home.'

Chapter 13

MATING TIME

Bushtail had encountered a badger on his lonely journey back to the City, just before he had come upon the awful awareness of what had happened as a result of the great killing, but little enough was his knowledge of them other than vague stories he had heard. Reynard assured him now that the badgers would not trouble them.

'A stupid lot really,' Reynard said. 'Leave some feathers outside, and the humans think the badgers have done it. But they'll share their place with thee and won't trouble thee. They be a fussy old lot though, for ever cleaning their bedding out, and all that sort of nonsense. Leave as much as a couple of old bones about the place and they'll clear off from there and go and live somewhere else.'

Bushtail was willing to take Reynard's word for the badgers' good character, but he was pleased, nevertheless, the following night, when Trotwood led him to a deep hole under the trunk of a fallen tree. If he was not going to be living in a community of foxes for the first time in his life, then better to be on his own than in too close proximity to a strange animal of whose ways he knew nothing. Before morning he came upon a nest of field mice, and followed that snack with the carcass of a plump pigeon, which he thought perhaps the humans had shot and had not been able to find. Reynard had told them to be ever on the look-out for such bounty. So much easier, he had said, than having to hunt for a meal and kill it yourself.

He slept all through the day and, when he stirred the following night, he was delighted to come upon a tree stump with news items, not only from Redvers and Rudyard, but from Reynard and Trotwood. The word was that Ivan had arrived with more than thirty City foxes, including more than a dozen cubs from three different City communities, and that Ranter had already formed a new committee. Ivan and his mates had said they would wait to see if there was anything doing during the mating season before making up their minds as to whether they would stay on or go back to the City. Meanwhile, two of Ranter's trusties had already set off for the City in search of more settlers.

There was something from far back in Bushtail's primaeval instinct which told him that this was the right life for him. He was greatly enjoying himself on his own, but still had the pleasure of meeting up occasionally with Redvers and Rudyard. Of the Ranter and Herman community they saw nothing, but heard much. The country foxes left their news items, and the constitution was a source of great amusement to them. They were also appalled at the way the Ranters, as they were now called, came and went, even by day, without any guile or caution. Redvers said he had always understood it to be instinctive to country foxes to take the utmost care before leaving or entering their den, and Reynard had not only confirmed it, but impressed on them the need to be especially alert at such times. It was, he said, the first thing which every vixen taught her cubs, and it gradually became clear to Bushtail that, however much Ranter and Herman dismissed the vixens as being of little consequence, they had a most important part to play in their very survival. There may not have been much threat to them from humans in the City, but there certainly was out here.

For some weeks the weather had been mild and damp, and the moon had been on the wane. Now, after nights of darkness, the sliver of a new moon appeared, the nights became crisp and clear, and there was white frost upon the fields. The news items on the tree stump said that Ranter's committee had met, and the mating schedule been decided. It came as no surprise to learn that Tinks had been allocated to Ranter, Nina to Herman, and Ginette to a leading member of the committee recently arrived from the City. Whilst all this was a source of further amusement to

Reynard, Trotwood and Blinker, it was as nothing to the hilarity when a news item was left by the incorrigible Ivan to the effect that Ranter was also in the process of considering arrangements for some of the country vixens.

Two nights later came the most startling news item of all. Bushtail had come to know the scent which Tinks had left so carefully for them along the way that he recognised it immediately again now. And the information she imparted, without any possibility of misunderstanding, was that she felt the season of the year upon her, and for any dog fox who was interested to be listening for her call.

Within the week, Bushtail was even more surprised, and not a little excited, to come upon similar messages from Nina and Ginette. So Tinks had initiated the other vixens into the mysteries of their kind, and it looked as if Ranter had sedition and open rebellion on his hands earlier than might have been expected in his new domain.

More than an exchange of messages was called for at this turn of events, and Rudyard was as pleased as Bushtail to discuss the possibilities. But, on this occasion, they failed to make contact with Redvers, or with Reynard and his two closest associates. Whatever was to be done they would have to decide between themselves.

Rudyard said later that it was as if all hell had been let loose. Bushtail said maybe that was an understatement.

The moon, waxing now, was riding high in a clear sky, and a great stillness was upon the woodland where the shadows fell. And it enveloped the fields and the hedgerows to the farm nestling against the hillside in the far distance, and from one window of which a light beamed out faintly. Distant though the homestead was, Bushtail, sharp of ear, heard a human voice call out, and a dog barked.

The sound of humans faded, and once more there was a pulsating silence, so loud that only the creatures of the wild could have understood it, and a strange, exciting scent was upon the frosty air. The world was hushed, and time, for long moments, stood still, until suddenly, from the middle distance, came the scream, the call, the beseeching of a vixen. Twice in quick succession the piercing call was repeated, and then, from three different parts, there came the staccato answers as the foxes barked.

89

Bushtail heard himself bark, too. He had known that call, as he had always felt he would know it in the freedom of the fields, and the thickets, and the moonlit glades of the woodland. He had vowed he would repay Ranter sooner or later, and the hour had come. He'd show him what he thought of his committee and his mating schedule. Had he been less excited as he loped through the wood he might have paused to consider whether there could also be others with the same intent.

Ranter was approaching Tinks just as Bushtail caught sight of her when, faster than light, a flurry of golden russet hurled itself in snarling fury from out of the shadows. Only three times did Reynard need to bite him, quick, vicious, snapping bites, for Ranter to know he was no match, and never could be, for this vulpine fiend. City living may have given him some strange ideas, but it had not entirely blunted his wits and sense of self preservation.

'Point of order,' Bushtail heard Rudyard say. 'You ain't seen nuffink yet, mate. An' don't ffink your turn'll come wiv her, cos a few more of us got ideas about this as well.'

'Hear, hear,' said Ivan.

Ranter, however, was already bleeding freely in two places from wounds to his neck, and stayed not to argue or to be goaded further, whilst not a fox moved as Reynard covered Tinks to his heart's content. Then, when he had done, the mayhem broke out, as Rudyard fought with Ivan, Bushtail started to fight with Trotwood before thinking better of it, Blinker made short work of Herman, and a couple of country foxes took issue with two recent arrivals from the City to such purpose as to make nonsense of Ranter's schedule.

When the whole lot of them had fought themselves to a standstill, Redvers came out of the shadows and, without any interference, sidled up to Tinks who had been watching from nearby. She called once, but there was no need, and Redvers was the next to couple with her.

For three nights Tinks called, and on the third night Bushtail's dream of her was fulfilled. But, by that time, other vixens were calling. According to Ranter's schedule, Nina was there for Herman, but, from the messages she had left on that most informative of tree stumps, it was known that Nina might well have had other ideas, and so had Blinker and Trotwood, whilst Ginette, too, was pleased to

90

accommodate a few most presentable country foxes who, as she said to Tinks and Nina later, had something more about them than the City types.

The moon had long since waned before the calling and the answering barks had dwindled to silence for the season. By that time, Bushtail had learned much, had the better of one country fox in fair fight, and covered, in addition to Tinks and Ginette, a far more acceptable country vixen than anything Ranter and his committee had ever allocated to him in the City. He decided he liked the country life, and it mattered not to him that the weather grew harder, and the nights became colder.

The mating season over, the more mundane realities of life still had to be faced. Day by day there was the need for food. Bushtail and Rudyard had learned much on the long and perilous journey from the City, and Redvers had an innate wisdom. Perhaps even more to their advantage, they had the goodwill of Reynard and the other country foxes. It was still, according to their ancestral law, every fox for himself, but the country foxes never failed to give them good advice and to leave news items on the old tree stump. The Ranters had no such benefits. All they had learned was too little, too late.

On their way out into the country, Ranter and his small contingent had gone on ahead, learning nothing from the devastation for others which their own stupidity had left in its wake. Most of those who had followed had been guided at various stages either by Rudyard or Redvers or by the Ivans. And now the Ranters were all out here in the country, with the weather making food more difficult to come by, and nobody to whom they could turn other than the pair of discredited fools who had led them into this situation, and whose authority was daily being set at nought as their community disintegrated into an indisciplined rabble.

In spite of all the boasting previously of his familiarity with the country, Herman had never learned to hunt, so there was little he could teach the others, even had he been minded to. There was also the other consideration that, in addition to this supposed experience of country life, he had the considerable accomplishment, or so he had always claimed, of having acquired an understanding of the humans. Now, however, those who had so far accepted such

91

posturing without question were beginning to see for themselves that Herman was most unlikely ever to be put to the test on this score, or have the chance to use such knowledge for the common good, for the simple reason that he was unlikely ever to be near enough to the humans to hear what they were saying. For that matter, they had already shown signs of coming to terms with the fact that they would be better advised to avoid the humans altogether anyway.

Such was the purport of the news items which Tinks left at the old tree stump from time to time, and Nina and Ginette also made the occasional contribution to the considerable knowledge of those who had good reason to keep a wary eye, nose and ear on the doings of these newcomers. Ivan and his three mercenaries had decided against returning to the City, but had resumed their travels in search of fresh interest, whilst the three vixens were showing increasing signs of being more than happy to adapt to the ways of the country. Not surprisingly, Ranter had branded them as traitors to the great cause, and the other City vixens were known to be exhibiting the same liberated tendencies.

Not only had they settled down after the brief, but intense euphoria of the mating season, but they had good reason to be concerned over the dangers which they sensed were inherent in the way they were now living. For they, too, in turn, could read the news items which the country foxes were leaving, and they found some of what they learned to be very disturbing. There was no definite word, as yet, of all the details, but certain it was that there was trouble. With the hard weather continuing, and food not easy to find, Ranter and Herman had organised a raid on a flock of sheep where the ewes were now heavy in lamb. That much Tinks knew for sure. Whitetip had told something of what had happened after the first great killing, and later she had learned from Bushtail and Rudyard the price the humans had exacted for that madness on the way from the City. She was learning fast, and she and the other two vixens were on the move in search of new earths away from Ranter's territory.

Chapter 14

TROUBLE AGAIN

Reynard had said earlier that it was fortunate for the growing cubs who came out from the City as part of Ranter's great settlement, that they had not arrived before the humans had been out hunting the cubs after harvest, because they would never have survived. Now, however, it was a different story, for the trouble which had been anticipated following the slaughter of the ewes was not long in coming.

Blinker it was who gave the first warning. He had long been known for his shortsightedness, but some there were who said that this could well be an advantage to him rather than any sort of handicap, since the foxes hunted for the most part by night, when sense of smell and hearing was far more important than what the hunter needed to see. Whatever Blinker may have lacked in sight he more than made up for with the other two senses, so that even though he was much more shortsighted than the average fox, he was also considerably sharper of ear and keener of scent.

Blinker, therefore, was the first to become aware of the advent of the humans, and he it was who raised the alarm. The Ranters had been so careless in their coming and their going, by day as well as by night, that the humans knew exactly where to find them. Bushtail, for his part, was quick to recognise the smell of the deadly steel. He would never forget how he had first been made aware of it on that miserable journey retracing his steps to the City when he had come upon the aftermath of the great killing.

The country foxes needed no further warning as to exactly what to expect, and they stayed well clear of the Ranters' territory until some nights later, when Bushtail was able to report that all smell of the steel traps and the wires had gone. It was not long before there were news items telling of the many foxes to have died, including most of the cubs from amongst the settlers who had arrived since harvest.

When the idea of the great move to the country had first been discussed back in the City it was the wise old Redvers who had pointed out the dangers of too many foxes living too close together. At that time, Herman had said that he knew of other woods and that the foxes would be able to split up. It came as no surprise, therefore, when the news left at the tree stump told of Herman and Ranter leading a few of those of their community who had survived, including two vixens who were in cub, to a wood which was a night's journey from their original settlement.

Ranter, according to the latest information, showed signs of having learned something at last, and the chosen band who accompanied him were now being much more careful to conceal their whereabouts. The humans, however, had no doubt been keeping a careful eye on the original territory, for a few nights later Herman was taken alive in one of their new devices and they took him away in a sack. His capture, it was reported, had come when he was visiting the foxes in the original territory for a discussion on the constitution. His replacement, according to the latest news items, was a fox by the name of Chopsy. Little was known of him except that Ranter had always considered his thinking and attitude to be politically correct.

The country foxes, however, had more important matters to occupy their minds. Not least were the worries as to how the behaviour of this influx from the City was going to affect their own lives.

For some time after the killing of the ewes the Ranters were not greatly in evidence, and there was nothing much by way of news items, apart from the fact that a couple of vixens had given birth to their cubs. The brief spell of hard weather had been followed by some high winds and heavy rain, and then the grass began to grow. But spring had not come yet. The birds were not yet nesting, the rabbits had not started to bring forth their young, and food was not all that easy to find. Occasionally there would be a bird which had been shot at by the humans and wounded, or killed and they had not been able to retrieve it. There was little to be found round the farms, because the humans seemed to be taking more care than ever and their buildings were tight shut by night.

In spite of all this, however, there were a few frogs and slugs and beetles in the damp places and the ditches, and Bushtail often reflected that life could have been much worse. These thoughts were in his mind, as he nosed along the growth at the base of a thick hedge, when he met Rudyard who was out on a similar mission.

The slim crescent of the pale moon was fading in a steel blue sky as the sun was rising in a red ball of fire beyond the far horizon.

'An' how you gettin' on, mate?' was Rudyard's cheerful greeting.

'Very well, indeed, Rudyard. Yes, it's a good life. In fact I was thinking about you the other day and wondering would you be going back to the City. Have you thought any more about it?'

'Nah. I ain't goin' back there, mate. They might have that Ranter's constitution. I don't want no more to do wiv that.'

'Well, the humans have got Herman. So that's a bit of good news.'

'A pity they can't get that Ranter as well, mate. He ain't no good. Maybe we could fix him ourselves some time.'

'Like we done that Arter, you mean?'

'Let's ffink about it. He ain't goin' to do no good out here, mate. He ain't goin' to have no vixens. He won't have nuffink. You want to hear old Tinks talk about him.'

'Tinks? Have you seen her lately?'

''Course I have. Brought her a rabbit, didn't I?'

'A rabbit? What you want to do that for?'

'For her cubs, o' course.'

'Has she got any cubs, then?'

''Course she has. Don't you know nuffink? Very disappointed in you, she is. Said you ain't been to see her, an' you ain't brought her nuffink for the cubs.'

'How many cubs has she got?'

95

'Six on 'em. Tinks says there's two by Reynard, one by Redvers, one of 'em is mine, one yours, an' she says one is Blinker's, so I reckons he can't be as shortsighted as that after all. An' Ginette ain't doin' so bad, neivver. She got six as well. One by Reynard, one by me, two by a couple o' these country foxes, an' she says as she knows who the uvvers is by as well. An' that's better than last time when she was in the City, cos she had that black un an' she never knew where he come from.'

Bushtail thought it could have been his lucky day, because he was on his way to look for Tinks when he came upon a rabbit which had just been killed by a weasel and, when he pounced, he nearly had the weasel as well.

When he found Tinks, she was in the sheltered corner of a field near the wood where she had her earth, and she was watching her cubs at play, what time she taught them how to hunt, and something of the lessons of survival. As far as Bushtail could see, they all looked alike and, if Tinks knew which was which, she must have been the only one who did. No doubt as they grew older their colouring would change, and then perhaps it would be easier to tell one from another.

Bushtail dropped the rabbit in front of her and told her he had been out specially to catch it for her.

'That was very kind of you, Bushtail,' she said. 'Most thoughtful. I suppose Rudyard told you he brought me one as well?'

'Yes, he mentioned something about it.'

'Good. I'm so glad about that. I thought perhaps he might. I asked him to, but I wasn't sure whether he would. Now if you'd be kind enough to tell some of the others, maybe I wouldn't have to do all the providing on my own around here.'

'I'm afraid that's how it is with us foxes, Tinks,' Bushtail said.

Some time later he discovered that Rudyard never had brought her a rabbit at all. He didn't hold it against him, for he recalled Rudyard saying to him a long time ago, 'It's all fair in love an' war, mate.' And then Bushtail chuckled as he remembered that, at the same time, it was none other than Rudyard who had warned him never to trust a female.

Bushtail had forgotten that two of Ranter's trusties had been

96

sent back to the City to collect more settlers, until Blinker left a message at the tree stump to say that another thirty of them had arrived. Bushtail had settled so well into his new life, and was so troubled by this latest development, that he had some idea how concerned and resentful the country foxes themselves must be.

Inevitably, the country foxes of the area now being affected felt the need to move out in search of new earths, to live as they had always lived, and as generations of their ancestors beyond number had lived before them, each to his or her own territory, for the most part at peace amongst themselves, scavenging and preying on other species where they could. With this latest development it meant that their whole way of life was under threat. Two communities from the City having been established already, there was no knowing where it could all end, and it was evident that something would have to be done.

Reynard had earlier doubted whether the Ranters would survive beyond the second winter, but he was the first to acknowledge that the country foxes themselves might yet have to take a hand in matters before they could expect life to return to normal. His own experience had clearly established that it was impossible to reason with Ranter, so it was now necessary to infiltrate his ranks to find out more exactly what was going on and, even more important, to learn something of any future plans.

The benign looking Blinker was delegated to make the initial approach. Having made contact, he turned up with Trotwood at the next meeting, where they both spoke with great enthusiasm of what they had seen, and came away committed to referring the matter to some of the country foxes whom they knew to have been equally impressed. They brought with them the news that trusted Comrades were already on their way back to the City, and it was confidently anticipated that at least another two new communities would be established before the next harvest.

Ranter, it seemed , was already familiarising himself with the seasons of the countryside. He admitted that they had perhaps been slightly indiscreet in the way they had previously moved about, but this was now being corrected and the Comrades were being instructed accordingly. To this end, it had been decided to vacate the area where so many of the Comrades had recently met such an untimely end, and to set up elsewhere. So, taking into account the areas which would be needed by the expected newcomers, they were really looking for three new areas in which to establish communities. Trotwood and Blinker had promised to put their local knowledge at the disposal of the committee to select suitable sites. It was a source of great satisfaction to all concerned that the four communities would come within the one tried and trusted constitution which had served them so well in the City.

Chapter 15

LESSONS TO LEARN

Elated beyond words at the prospect of Trotwood and Blinker joining him and helping him to enlarge his empire, Ranter even went so far as to promise them at least one place on the committee, especially if they were able to bring enough new members with them. As it transpired, it was not long before the tree stump carried a news item which suggested that things were not going according to plan.

Soon afterwards Blinker reported that, contrary to Ranter's dreams and fondest expectations, the more recent settlers showed no sign of submitting to his directions, and were clearly out of control. It had come as a nasty shock to him, but he was now without the erstwhile valued support of the so sadly departed Herman, whilst Chopsy was proving not only to be inadequate, but to be showing distinct signs of building up a faction of his own.

Possibly, given time, Ranter could have manipulated something to bring things under control, but the weather conspired against him. Whereas originally the first settlers had been enthusiastic for the move into the country, with every intention of living according to the constitution, and were correct in their thinking and their attitudes, these more recent arrivals were scornful of the constitution and were, Ranter had told Trotwood, quite impossible. When the weather turned suddenly cold it was too much for them.

As so often happens, the weather had flattered only to deceive. Spring had not come. Suddenly a cold wind blew from the north east, and snow fell. Even then survival was possible. There was always the occasional sickly lamb, or the chance carcass of a ewe that had died and which some indifferent farmer had been in no hurry to bury. It was not unknown sometimes to be able to dig up a carcass that had not been buried deep enough. The odd hen here and there did not usually attract a fury of vengeance, nor did the taking of a few piglets where possible. Always, from time to time, there would be the afterbirth when a cow calved, or a ewe lambed, out-of-doors.

But all this was not good enough for the Johnny-come-latelies, as Rudyard called them.

Young lambs were at their mothers' heels in the field within easy distance, and Ranter's latest settlers killed on an unheard of scale. There could never be any doubt as to the retribution which would follow, and within a matter of hours there was a message left at the tree stump to say that Ranter had gone into hiding on his own, but that Blinker would be able to locate the fugitive as soon as it was necessary.

Heavy rain had washed away the melting snow as quickly as it had come, but it had been too late to help Ranter in any possible hope he might ever have entertained of convincing his new followers of the suicidal folly of what they were doing.

Before the ever alert and reliable Blinker had any scent of the humans who were expected to come any day now with their steel traps and wires, there was other human activity, and Blinker said it was the humans on their horses who would be coming with their great dogs. They had not been that way since the few humans had been out with the young hounds to hunt for the cubs after harvest, but they would be coming in greater numbers any day now.

That same evening Redvers left word for Bushtail and Rudyard that he wished to see them. They had no fear of the humans with the steel traps and the wires, because the country foxes all knew to stay away from the two areas of the Ranters until the danger was over but, if the hounds were coming, Redvers said, then other possibilities presented themselves. Bushtail met Rudyard on the way, and Redvers was waiting for them when they reached a high bank of gorse bushes near his own den.

Much as he was enjoying this new life in the country, Bushtail sometimes missed the companionship of the more communal life of the City, and it was a good feeling to be

100

together like this for a while with the two foxes with whom he had now shared so many dangers.

Without preamble, Redvers said he had been talking to Reynard who had said that they had to get rid of Ranter.

'That's a good idea, mate,' Rudyard said. 'Me an' Bushtail here was sayin' the same ffing the last time as we met.' He had always hated Ranter.

'I'm pleased to hear it, my friends. Reynard has a plan and he explained it to me. I agreed with him entirely, but suggested slight alterations.'

'You did?'

'Well, the plan remains the same, but I suggested that you should take part. I reckon we owe it to these country foxes because by coming here like we have we've threatened their whole way of life. Don't think it's some big talk about principles or anything like that. Far from it. That's never been our nature. But you know I was against this business right from the time when it was first talked about back in the City. And if it hadn't been for us the whole crazy scheme would have been a disaster anyway. Now that we're here I reckon we ought to lend a hand for our own benefit. As long as that fool Ranter is about the place we'll never be safe.'

'Dear me,' said Bushtail. 'You're talking like our friend Rudyard here. You make it sound as if you're planning to stay here as well. Aren't you going back to the City after all?'

'No, I think not. I've had many talks with Reynard, and he keeps saying the same thing nearly every time I see him. Redvers come home, he keeps saying. Redvers come home. And I think maybe he's right. Happiness is within us. Long ago I came to realise that if you can't be happy here, then you won't be happy there. And this is where we belong. The City isn't right for us, and never could be.'

'Well, that's wonderful news. You know I hoped you'd stay. There's so much you can do to help us and advise us.'

'I don't know about that. But, as long as you're willing, Reynard'll be more than pleased to have you in on his plan, and I told him I could rely on you.'

'Wot's the plan wiv him then, Mate?' Rudyard asked.

'I think,' said Redvers, 'it would be better for him to explain it to you himself. He's a very wise and cunning old fox, and he's got it all worked out for Ranter to be killed by the hounds. Personally, I reckon he's caused so much trouble for these good country foxes that it's too good a death for him.'

'Too good a death!' said Bushtail. 'It's a terrible death, isn't it?'

'Not according to Reynard. He reckons it's the noblest way for a fox to die. One snap of the jaws from a hound and he's dead, Reynard says. By the time they tear him apart afterwards he knows nothing about it. Not like the creatures we kill, and torment them if we can before they die, and delight to see their suffering.'

'Course we do,' Rudyard said. 'Stands to reason, don't it. Have a real bit o' fun wiv 'em.'

'Sure,' Redvers said. 'But for me, I want to go quick. I hope when my time comes it'll be with one quick snap from a hound's jaws. I'd rather that than a lingering death in the City, or out here in a trap, or by poison, or be shot at and be dying in agony in the bushes for days on end. I want to go quick.'

'So, when do we see Reynard?' Bushtail asked.

'He's waiting for you now, if you want to see him. Go down to that gate and you'll find a scent posting for you. See you tomorrow, and good luck.'

For much of the previous day and throughout the night there had been a heavy mist, but that had cleared at last, the atmosphere was mild, and the ground was damp. Now, at first light, Reynard said the conditions were perfect, especially if they could keep as far as possible to the grassland and avoid the ploughed fields. It would suit their own purpose to perfection, and the humans would be delighted, because the hounds would be able to pick up the scent so easily they would have a really good run.

Bushtail was filled with admiration afterwards when he understood how Reynard had planned out every move, and yet made it sound so simple. And to think that an idiot such as Ranter had had the audacity to say the country foxes were stupid. Redvers, even in his City days, had known better than that.

The success of their entire plan, Reynard had said, was to make absolutely certain that the hounds were not allowed to get anywhere near either of the Ranters' two communities, for if that were to happen there would be complete chaos. The humans with their steel traps and wires, and maybe even with poison and with their guns, would deal with them in their own good time. Of that he was certain. Their own concern was with Ranter.

The estimable Blinker had long since located his whereabouts and established that he was staying put. Reynard had said he had to admit to a sneaking admiration for him, for it looked as if he had shown signs of learning something at last. But, as usual, it was still a case of too little too late. The fool still hadn't enough sense to go to earth, and he would be an easy quarry to flush out. Apparently he had gone by a most circuitous route, doubling back on his tracks more than once, until he had finished up after a hard night's travelling within close proximity to his two communities. It thus made life easy for Blinker, who was close enough to keep them informed of any and every development.

Finally, Reynard had told them, since this was something new to them, to remember that a fox would never outrun a hound. The hound was faster and had greater stamina. The secret was to avoid them by stealth and cunning. So sure of everything was he in all he had said that he had given them a feeling of complete confidence and wellbeing. Nor did they have long to wait.

By mid-morning the humans on their horses had assembled. Scarcely had they set off when Reynard was seen to steal quietly from cover, a horn blew as he went away, the first hound challenged, and the rest of the pack gave tongue. For five fields Reynard stayed in view and the hounds went with heads up in full cry until, after four hedges and a wide ditch, they were closing on him fast when he came to a field where he ran through a flock of sheep. The sheep were not disturbed by Reynard, but at sight of the hounds the sheep scattered and the hounds lost the scent. Following this check, by the time the dogs found scent again it had changed and they were on a fresh fox. A fine sight to be sure, Redvers was with his rich red coat and the white tip to his tail with the distinctive black ring round it, and a fair run he gave them, too, until he came to a wide, slowly flowing stream. By now it was clear that things were going badly for him, but he was able to enter the water and, by the time he came out on the opposite bank well downstream, the hounds had lost the scent and checked again.

It was at this point that Rudyard was seen to break cover and go away. Once more the hounds gave tongue, but they lost him when he crossed a road and doubled back twice, by which time they were close on the scent of Trotwood. And Trotwood gave the hounds every encouragement until he came to a copse where they lost him and changed to Bushtail who was waiting for them.

This, Reynard had said, although only a small part of the plan, was still one of the most important. The country foxes had all been warned to keep well away from the copse that day, but there was no knowing what some of Ranter's stupid crowd might do, particularly as it was close to their own area. So there could well be other foxes there, and it was vital for Bushtail to ensure that the hounds stayed close enough not to lose scent of him for one moment. When Reynard had explained this to him originally, Bushtail had felt a glow of pride to have been entrusted with such an important role. Now, at one point, when the hour had come, he thought he had almost pushed his luck too far but, by the time he came out beyond the copse, the hounds had lost him momentarily and had changed to Blinker's scent on the last stage to lead them to Ranter.

A cunning enough place in many ways it was which Ranter had found for himself, but by no means suitable for his purpose in this, his moment of extremity. As he panicked and broke from cover, Rudyard, who was determined to be in at the kill, was there again, and that had been no part of the plan. But Blinker kept his head, loped away into the undergrowth and, as the great baying hounds closed in, Rudyard shot past a bewildered Ranter to leave him at their mercy, and said as he went, 'Point of order, mate. Now tell 'em all about yer constitution.'

Chapter 16

WHO'S BOSS?

Not for one moment was there any doubt amongst the country foxes as to what the result of the ravages amongst the sheep would be. Reynard's plan, so cleverly conceived, and so efficiently executed, had kept the hounds away from both areas now occupied by the City settlers and had rid the country foxes of the pestilential Ranter. All that the plan had achieved for the humans had been to give them a good day's sport with a marvellous run and a kill at the finish. That could not in any way assuage the wrath engendered by the slaughter of so many lambs and a number of ewes. For that, most certainly, a price would have to be paid.

It was not long before Blinker reported a strong human presence, but no word was there from Bushtail of any scent of the dreaded steel, and that could mean only one thing. It would be something else this time.

The country foxes, highly apprehensive, were more than usually suspicious, and Reynard's message was possibly superfluous. Even so, he impressed on them the need for extra caution. Above all, he urged them to stay away from any carcasses and carrion, however tempting some of it might be during this time when food was not yet plentiful. If any of them had their doubts, the wisdom of Reynard's caution came home to them most forcibly before long, when so many of the City foxes were seen to be dying in agony.

There were, however, those of the first settlers who had begun to learn something from their experiences in these new surroundings and had survived. It was some days before there was any definite news, because Blinker and Trotwood were not too sure to what extent their own parts in the death of Ranter would have been suspected. Eventually Blinker left a message to say that he had again made contact with the remnants of the two Ranter communities. It was clear that the settlers knew little of what had really happened, apart from having heard that he and Trotwood had been involved in the chase, and they had congratulated him on their marvellous escape.

But if it had been thought that with the demise of Ranter the country foxes had resolved all their difficulties, they were due for an unpleasant surprise. Chopsy had assumed power and, even though not as wordy as Ranter, or as his name implied, he most certainly meant business.

He had gathered all the survivors to form one new small community and, having recognised their vulnerability if they remained where they were, had asked Blinker and Trotwood for the benefit of their advice in selecting yet one more new site. They found him an area, not much frequented by the country foxes, where the badgers lived in some numbers. Even if they had not been able to explain it, both Blinker and Trotwood, with their in-bred native cunning, thought that could have been a sensible thing to do.

It was in this place, selected for him by those who knew the area and the ways of the country, that Chopsy set up his new community, adapting their constitution to the changed pattern of life in their new surroundings. There was to be less emphasis on the constitution and such strict control of their own day-to-day conduct, and far more on enlightening the country foxes and showing them the folly of their ways. No opportunity must be lost to bring them closer to the humans, and to show them that the humans really would care for them and think more kindly of them if they could be prevailed upon to change their whole way of life, which meant living in community. After all that had happened recently this seemed to the country foxes to be slightly puzzling.

Reynard, having come to the conclusion that the City foxes were even bigger fools than they had seemed in the first place, and realising how serious this new development could be, was still giving the matter a great deal of consideration, when a startling news item was left at the tree stump. Somewhat unusually, there was no indication as to the identity of who had left it, and Reynard came to the conclusion that there must be at least one disaffected member of Chopsy's community, one who had also learned how the country foxes left their messages. Be that as it may, and he thought the possibility was perhaps of some considerable importance, this news item was such as to warrant serious attention, not only because of its purport, but by virtue of the undisguised terms in which it had been couched.

Herman was back. That was what the news item said. Yes, truly, the wise, the far-seeing, the incomparable Herman, who had helped to lay the plans for their great adventure, who had been there at Ranter's right hand, who had advised and encouraged and guided all along the way, who knew the language of the humans, who was familiar with the ways of the country. The great, the wise, the truly incomparable Herman. He was back with them once again. All was not lost. Herman was back.

Before ever there had been time for this news item to be assimilated and properly assessed, it became clear that, whatever the evident excitement of its purveyor, his enthusiasm was not shared by at least one of the City foxes. Chopsy himself, no less, saw no cause for rejoicing. For Chopsy had already taken control. And Chopsy had no intention of letting go. Blinker passed on the news that they were now witnessing a tremendous power struggle and there was no knowing how things would develop.

It was not long before Blinker reported that even the hardliners of the old guard were having to be careful to safeguard their own crumbling influence, for Chopsy had already formed his own new committee before Herman had returned. Almost their first decision had been to send a trusted comrade back towards the City to meet any further newcomers on the way, to suggest they should delay their move, and then lead them to some new area where a fresh start could be made and where Chopsy would contact them as soon as possible.

A few nights later it was Trotwood who paid the City foxes a visit, and the news item he left on the tree stump afterwards was more startling than any it had ever carried in all its years of service as a posting place for countless generations of country foxes.

The first item of interest was that the message saying that Herman had returned had been left by Herman himself. The vanity of the fool was of no consequence. What made him dangerous was the fact that by some means or other he had become privy to their methods of communication. That alone meant that he would need to be disposed of. And sooner rather than later. But the impact of the other news item which followed it caused messages to be sent to posting places for all the foxes over a wide area. Herman, it was reported, before being released by the humans, had been fitted with a collar with some device which would make it possible for them to follow all his movements. More startling still was the fact that he was now claiming that he had understood what the humans had been saying, but Trotwood said he had failed in his attempt to use this knowledge as a weapon in his power struggle with Chopsy. Trotwood also left a message for Reynard saying he wanted to meet him.

Following that meeting, Reynard made a point of seeing as many foxes in the area as possible rather than risk leaving news items which Herman could have picked up about himself. For, let there be no doubt about it, Reynard told Redvers, Bushtail and Rudyard when he met them by the steep bank where the gorse grew, Herman was now a far greater danger to them than Ranter had ever been. Ranter had been a temporary nuisance, and now Chopsy was. But they could see him off whenever they felt like it without too much trouble, whereas this Herman business was far, far more serious.

It was a long story which Reynard had to tell them and he admitted he was not sure how much of it to believe himself. The most important part of his talk with Trotwood, he told them, was that Herman had wanted to see him if possible, and so Reynard had met him. The fact that Herman was a fool and that Reynard did not like him was neither here nor there. It had been clear from the outset, Reynard said, that Herman had asked to meet him because he was in trouble. He had lost out to Chopsy over leadership of their community and did not even have a place on the new committee.

'Well, I strung'n along with talk about that for a time,' Reynard said, 'and then he started to tell me what had happened with the humans, and that's what I don't know whether to believe or not, or at any rate how much of it. He certainly got this collar round his neck and he reckons there's a little thing in it that means the humans can keep track on him wherever he goes or whatever he does.'

'Marvellous,' said Rudyard. 'That's all I need to hear. An' wot else was there wiv him?'

'Patience, my friend. That's not the half of it.'

The woodland was very still that night and scarcely a breeze was there to rustle in the trees. And then Reynard told them a story, the like of which they had never heard. Even Redvers, who had been renowned for his wonderful gift for hearing, and remembering, and telling again the stories handed down from generation to generation by the foxes from long, long ago, was lost for words.

Herman had told Reynard how he had been taken alive by the humans and handled gently, fed well and treated most kindly, just as he had been when he was young before they had released him into the wild, when instinct had led him back to the City where he had been born. He had gone on then to admit that he had forgotten much of the language of the humans, but it soon came back to him, and he had understood some of what they were saying.

There had been some talk amongst them of humans, who were not friends of the foxes, and who collected them in vans from the City and took them away to be killed. Now, however, there were other vans with people who brought the foxes to the country so that they could have a nice life. But apparently not all the humans were as kind as that, or as those he had remembered from his younger days, and this was a possibility of which Redvers had warned right from the start. Now, however, things were changing. There were those who said that foxes must only be shot, or caught in the steel traps, or even poisoned, and never chased or killed by the humans on their horses and with the big dogs. And then Herman had gone on to tell an even more remarkable story. These laws were to be made, he said, by people who had come to live in the country from the City, in the same way as the foxes had done. And the almost unbelievable part of it all was that the country people had made these City people welcome and now had no idea how to get rid of them.

'If you asks me, mate,' Rudyard grinned, 'these humans ain't half as smart as us foxes, an' I ain't half glad I joined up wiv you lot.'

'He'll have to go,' Redvers said.

'Indeed,' said Reynard. 'And maybe it's even more serious than thee'rt thinking. According to this Herman, if he can be believed, the humans seemed to understand that he wasn't afraid of 'em, and they hoped he might be easy to catch again or even to come back to 'em for food. They let'n out for a day or two and he kept going back for food, so then they took'n back to the wood and they're waiting to see if he'll go back to 'em again. And he's planning to do this. But all the time he's moving about among us they'll know what he's doing.'

'So wot's to do wiv him, mate?' Rudyard asked.

Reynard gave them a little time to think of the seriousness of the situation. Then he said that Blinker and Trotwood had done well in directing Chopsy to set up his new community amongst the badgers. It would be no bad idea to direct some of the humans' attention towards the badgers for a change. But on one point he was adamant. This was no job for any of the former City foxes. He and the others were pleased they had settled amongst them, and they had valued their help in getting rid of Ranter, but this was a different matter. This required experience, and he did not want to see any mishap befall them, nor could they afford to take the slightest possible risk of things going wrong. That was why he was telling them all about it, he said, so that they would know to keep out of the way, the same as so many of the country foxes had needed to do on that memorable day that Ranter had died.

There could be no question that Reynard would know how to handle whatever plan his cunning brain had contrived, but there seemed to be so many outside influences these days which could interfere with life as he and their forbears had known it since time out of mind. One such occurred now, and it could not have happened better for him if he had spent a lifetime planning it. Whereas it could have destroyed

110

his scheme, he turned it with fiendish cunning to his own advantage.

He had sent word to Herman that he would see him the following night to put certain proposals to him. Throughout the following day, as he dozed, Reynard turned over in his mind the details of his plan.

Late in the afternoon it happened, and the trusty Blinker was the first to scent and spread the news. A van had arrived, been driven into a field near the wood, and a couple of humans had released a dozen foxes. Before the van had left, Bushtail had alerted Redvers, and the pair of them had recognised the familiar scent of one of the City vans. So there was some truth at any rate in the story that Herman had told. City foxes they were, none too healthy looking, and completely bewildered as they wandered in search of shelter.

Reynard needed to know no more. As dusk was falling he sought them out, told them where the other City foxes had settled, and led them, too, away to the far wood where the badgers were. Apart from anything else, their arrival would come as a nasty surprise for Chopsy. Meanwhile, Bushtail and Trotwood were sent in search of Herman to tell him that Reynard needed to see him on a matter of the greatest urgency.

It was the following night before they heard the end of the story, and then Reynard gave them the brief details and told them how, in the event, it had been unbelievably simple. Herman, he said, never would have had the brains or cunning to succeed as a leader of foxes living in the country. Reynard had met him and told him that it was important that he should find out for himself whether there were any of his former supporters amongst the newcomers. He had also impressed on him that after what had been happening lately it was more than likely that the unfriendly humans would come in search of them. So it was equally important for Herman to find a good place to hide securely.

Trotwood had been at hand, Reynard said, when he arrived with Herman, and they led him down to the end of the deepest earth where two badgers had their set. The sow had three cubs with her and she would not let the foxes pass, so Reynard and Trotwood annoyed her until she grunted in anger, and then the boar came.

'They be like that, them badgers,' said Reynard. 'Real fools when it comes to family, sticking to their own mates and all that sort of nonsense.'

And by the time her mate came, the badger sow was mad, and the boar was even madder, and there was Herman trapped between them and he wouldn't live to tell the tale. But, said Reynard, he and Trotwood had lived to tell it, because that was the way they had planned it in the first place.

Chapter 17

SEEK AND YE SHALL FIND

There was great amusement, as well as much satisfaction, over the manner of Herman's elimination. From first to last the plan had been a complete success. And now, for good measure, Herman's body, with the leather collar round his neck, was stuck far down amongst the badgers in one of the deepest earths any of them had ever known. So now the humans would have to dig, and that would disturb the badgers and annoy them.

Far better than disturbing the stupid old badgers, however, was the thought that it would annoy some of the humans. Herman had told them that the humans had been arguing amongst themselves and some of them were even more friendly to the badgers than they were to the foxes. The ones who had put the collar on his neck had been arguing with some of the others, and none of them had anything to do with those who didn't like the foxes and who came hunting them on their horses and with their great hounds.

There was one occasion when those who were friends of the foxes had been waving flags or something, and shouting at one another, and there had been a great deal of trouble altogether and they were always arguing with one another, so Herman had said.

113

Of course, it was no good believing everything Herman had told them, but it had to be admitted that some of what he had said had turned out to be true.

Whatever happened next, one thing was certain. The humans would be coming in search of the collar with its device for them to know where Herman was and to follow what he was doing. They would be more than a little puzzled to think of him down at the bottom of a badger's set and maybe they would think he was stuck. Yes, most certainly they would have to dig, no matter how much trouble it caused.

There was much amusement amongst the foxes, and some very interesting news items and messages were being left on the old tree stump night after night. Then, after about a week, the humans came. Those who had put the collar on Herman had come to dig, but those who were waving the flags were shouting at them. Some more humans were standing back laughing about the others, and Reynard said afterwards that they were the ones who were no friends of the foxes. He said he couldn't be sure, but the scent that they had left where they had been standing was quite definitely the same scent which was left by those who came out to hunt them on their horses and with their great hounds. As a humorous afterthought he said it was almost a pity that Herman couldn't be brought back to tell them what the humans had been saying.

There was one good thing to have come out of it, Reynard said, and that was that the humans knew now, even if they hadn't known before, where Chopsy and company were. It would hardly be long before they would be out on their horses and with their great hounds, or with their steel traps and their wire. Chopsy and his mates would not be a nuisance to the country foxes for much longer. They had seen Arter off for themselves, along with Ranter and Herman. There need be no doubt or concern about Chopsy. He could quite safely be left to the humans.

Whatever had happened between the humans after all their shouting, they had not done any digging, but the foxes were careful to keep an eye, and a ear, and a nose on all that was going on. Not surprisingly, Blinker it was who had scent of something being amiss, but Rudyard said that it didn't need a nose like Blinker's to lead them to the source of the trouble.

It had no doubt been too much for the badgers as Herman's body had started to decay, and they had dragged his stinking carcass out along with their old bedding. So the laugh was no longer on the badgers. All it needed now was for a human to come and collect the collar with the device in it, and then they could put it on some other fox they were able to catch. It would be no trouble to catch Chopsy or one of the fools with him, and who knew how much trouble that would cause? For the time being Chopsy and some of the Comrades were making a meal of Herman. By the time the humans arrived there would be nothing much left apart from his bare bones. And that collar with the device in it. The humans would know it had moved and they would be there any time now to find out what was happening.

Reynard it was who decided that if it were not exactly an emergency, then certainly something needed to be done about it. It required but few messages on the old tree stump and elsewhere before he and Blinker and Trotwood were joined by Redvers, Rudyard and Bushtail.

In some detail he pointed out to them what was involved and what they should be trying to do. Even if one of the foxes could get hold of the collar before the humans came, there would still be the need to get rid of it, and that was something which would be beyond them.

'We must think fast,' he said, 'and we must act fast if we're going to stay on top.'

'Wot you means, mate,' Rudyard said, 'is that time is of the essence. You ain't ffinkin' correct since some on our Comrades have gorn an' left us. Or been took from us as you might say by 'orrible accidents, most gory an' 'orrible.'

Redvers put his big ears forward. 'Did you say on top, Reynard? On top?'

'Indeed I did. We must do all we can to stay on top.'

'I thought for one foolish moment that you said on top.'

'Yes, of course, that's what I said. And that's what I meant. We must try to stay on top.'

'What a splendid idea! That's the answer.'

'What's the answer?'

'To stay on top. The answer's in the trees.'

'The trees!' Reynard said. 'What can that mean? The trees! Why talk in puzzles, my old friend?'

'Even in death,' Redvers grinned, 'the late Comrade Herman speaks to us. Amongst other things he told us about the humans, he said that not only were there those who loved the foxes and the badgers and the rabbits, and even the rats and the mice and the adders, but there were also those who loved the trees.'

'But Redvers, my friend, what do trees have to do with it?'

'I'll tell you. Those who love the trees make sure that before any human can cut down a tree, many other humans must be asked about it first.'

'Well?' Reynard said, and Redvers had to chuckle again, because he had always said 'well' himself when he couldn't think of anything else to say.

'Well,' Redvers said, 'how would it be if we picked up Herman's collar and put it high up at the top of a tree?'

There was a long silence amongst the other foxes, and then Reynard said, 'Redvers, old friend, there's no need to say come home. Thee'rt home. As a country fox I almost hate to say it, but thee'rt smarter than any of us. Thee'rt home, my friend. Thee'rt home.'

Rudyard it was who came up with what was considered to be the final touch to Redvers' splendid idea, and he therefore claimed the honour of putting the delightful refinement into operation. In any case, he argued, he had done more tree climbing than the rest of them, and Redvers said that it sounded just about the sort of crazy thing he would delight in doing anyway, even if he had never climbed a tree in his life.

In a valley which was distant no more than a short night's journey there was a small colony of herons, and close to the river they nested in the highest of the high trees.

'Them big birds wiv the long legs an' long necks,' Rudyard said. 'They'd be pleased to see me I reckons. Wot d'you ffink, mates?'

'Thee'rt mad,' Reynard said. 'No fox have ever been known to climb as high as that.'

'There got to be a first time for everyffink. An' them humans could never do it. Stands to reason, don't it? Too big an' heavy, that's wot, mate. So once Herman's collar's up in one of them big nests them humans would never get it unless they chopped the tree down. An' how could they do that if they was to ffink as Herman was in the nest wiv his collar on? Stands to reason, don't it?'

Bushtail claimed the privilege of going with Rudyard on the grounds that they had done so much together on the journey from the City, and therefore had a proper understanding if danger threatened.

The sun had set long since when they reached the Chopsy territory, but no sign or sound of Chopsy or his Comrades disturbed their senses. As darkness closed in they could see that scarcely anything remained of Comrade Herman, and either Chopsy or one of his mates had obligingly ripped the collar from what had once been his neck. Bushtail put his nose to it and, as he did so, his sharp hearing picked up the faint sound of a bleep or tick, like that of some underground insect. It was such a sound which always told the foxes where to dig.

'What d'you make of that?' Bushtail said.

'Nuffink, mate. It's them humans. That ffing wotever they calls it as they puts in there to know where Comrade Herman has gorn. An' now they'll know, won't they, mate? He's gorn an' got hisself up into one of them big nests wiv them birds wiv the long legs an' long necks. Or he will be if we don't stand here messin' about. I reckon them humans'll be here tomorrer.'

It was a leisurely journey on a pleasant moonlit night which took them to the heronry, and they reached there as dawn was breaking on a misty morning which promised another good day. The spring growth flourished, but the leaves on the trees had not as yet hidden from sight the massive bundles of sticks which were the herons' nests. The songbirds had awakened and were greeting the day when Bushtail and Rudyard arrived, and then the bird-song died and changed to calls of alarm. Way up high, great grey herons swayed on slender branches, whilst some came and went on slow-moving black-tipped wings. Bushtail looked up and the prospect made him dizzy. He had climbed trees in the parks of the City many a time, but never anything like this.

He dropped the collar he had been carrying, Rudyard grinned, picked it up with his teeth without a word, twitched his tail a few times as though winding himself up, leapt with a mighty leap up to the lowest branch, and began to climb.

With his tail wrapped round himself, Bushtail sat on his haunches and watched every move as Rudyard went, but with one ear forward and one back to pick up every sound that might tell of danger. Already the croaking note of the herons' call had turned to one of alarm, and there was increasing agitation as Rudyard went up and up and ever upwards, using his bushy tail now to help his balance. High, high he was, almost at the slender top of the tree, balanced precariously on the slightest of branches above one of the great nests, when Bushtail saw him sway, and then somehow, almost defying belief, ease himself down none too gently, but gently enough not to do any damage, into the nest. Great indeed was the commotion in the heronry and the agitated croaking delighted Bushtail's ears. How good it was to spread panic amongst such creatures. Rudyard sent two fluffy youngsters crashing down and Bushtail made a quick, welcome meal of them. He doubted not that Rudyard would have had a few for himself. And then the humans came.

Downwind of them Bushtail was, and such was the noise everywhere by this time that his moist nose scented them long before his ears had sound of them.

Three of them there were but, by the time they arrived at the foot of Rudyard's tree, Bushtail had moved stealthily away into the undergrowth and by great good fortune found himself in a position from which he could see the movements both of the humans and of the lofty Rudyard. He found himself thinking what a shame it was that Redvers could not have been there to see it all for himself as there followed such an episode as would surely go down in the fox lore and legend so beloved of the old fox. Especially as the scheme had been the brainchild of his own cunning in the first place.

Bushtail had no great fear of these humans, because no dogs were with them and, according to all reports so far, these humans who were after the collar appeared to be from amongst those who were friendly to the foxes, even though they did not seem to be friendly with the humans who went about waving flags and shouting when the ones after the collar wanted to dig down to the badger set. Bushtail decided that humans must be a daft lot altogether.

He did not understand what they were saying, but he could tell they were very excited. Nor could he understand what the things were which they carried, but from what Herman had once said they had things for making pictures and it looked as if this could be what one of them was doing. One of them had things over his ears and seemed to be listening, and the other was holding something to his eyes and looking up at Herman as they no doubt thought. They would never see from that distance that it was Rudyard's mask that was sticking out over one side of the nest, any more than they could tell it was Rudyard's brush protruding over the other. The important thing was that they had found where Herman's collar was and would be able to hear the ticking device.

For a long time the humans talked and pointed, until the sun was high in the sky, and still the herons came and went with their croaking call, and still greatly distressed. Then a strange thing happened. Bushtail knew the scent long before she appeared, but even so he was still greatly surprised when Tinks trotted boldly across the clearing with her six cubs.

They had grown and had started to take on their adult colouring since last he had seen them. If Tinks had been the only one who could have known which was which when he had seen them previously, there was no question now, and Redvers' cub, for one, stood out clearly with his rich red colouring and the distinctive black ring round the clear white tip of his tail. At sight of the humans they stopped at a word from Tinks and stood as though frozen. Then one of the humans moved, and Tinks and her litter disappeared into the bushes. For a long time the humans waited patiently until, eventually, young Redvers appeared on his own. Then two more of the cubs came into the clearing and chased each other, before all three once more disappeared.

So the game went on until the humans became impatient and at last went away to the area where Tinks and her cubs were. Faster than Bushtail could have believed such a thing to be possible, Rudyard came down the tree and joined Bushtail in his secluded hiding place.

Apparently having failed to find Tinks, the humans returned. There was no longer any sight of a fox up above, but the human with things on his ears nodded and made noises and seemed pleased. As long as they could hear the device in Herman's collar ticking away, high up in the heron's nest, they were no doubt well satisfied.

The herons had settled down at last and, as Rudyard and Bushtail made their way home, long after sunset and when the moon was rising, Rudyard told Bushtail of old Redvers' cunning strategy.

'Twas he was the one wot done it, mate,' Rudyard said. 'Stands to reason, don't it. No takin' chances wiv him. He's crafty, mate. Left a message for Tinks to tell her 'twould be a good chance to teach them cubs she got. How to cause a diversion or distraction was wot he said, or some long word like that, an' old Reynard said as Redvers was gettin' more cunnin' all the time.'

For one whole moon afterwards, and long after that, news items were being left at the old tree stump. They were nothing particularly exciting except to say that the humans were still patiently watching the heron's nest, and various foxes were taking it in turns to put in the occasional appearance in the clearing to keep the humans interested.

Chapter 18

THEN CHARLEY ARRIVED

With the coming of summer, young Charley also arrived. Unknown though he was to the country foxes, his advent was not unexpected, because news items had been posted here and there along the way. Furthermore, Bushtail and Rudyard had been helped by his father, the gipsy type they had known as the foxy chal. He it was who had brought them a most helpful message from Whitetip, and had shown much goodwill towards them on their long and hazardous journey from the City.

It was a fragrant evening, and Bushtail was making his way along the bank of the stream in search of frogs or whatever small life might be on offer by way of a tasty morsel.

Charley, like his father, looked an ordinary sort of fox, with his yellow brown colouring and black points, but there was also a devil-may-care, adventurous air about him. Bushtail sensed straightaway that he was a wanderer.

'Kushto bokht, prale,' Charley said.

'So you'll be young Charley,' Bushtail said, in reply to the newcomer's Romany greeting. 'How's your old man these days?'

'Gone tramping the toby for the summer.'

Throughout the day the long grass had rippled quietly in the gentle breeze, but now the world was at peace and the birds had fallen silent for their night's rest.

'It's good to meet you,' Bushtail said, 'but what brings you our way?'

'Interested to meet thee. Heard about the way some of the flatties killed the little gry and started a whole heap of trouble.'

'Flatties?'

'Sure. The City lot. Killed the little gry.'

'The pony, you mean?'

'That was a big mistake, pal.'

'Indeed it was, but we've learned a lot since then. At least, some of us have.'

'Sure. We heard how thee got rid of that carver.'

'Carver?'

'Cheat, pal. Cheat. That Ranter. One of the flash coves. That was his moniker, wasn't it? Bad cess to him.'

'Oh, yes, We fixed him, and we fixed Herman'

'Sure. We heard about that as well.'

'And what else have you heard?'

'The word is that some of thee settled down. After that, Whitetip gave me the line on young Tinks.'

'Young Tinks?'

'Sure. The word is that Tinks had two vixens in her lot this last time and thee'rt the father of young Tinks.'

'Is that so?'

'Straight up, pal. And I've come to see what the strength is. Maybe I'll come back this way clicketting time and try my luck with her. Could thee put a word in for me, pal?'

'I don't know that I've got much influence like that. From what I could see of it last time round it's every fox for himself.'

'Theer't learning, pal. Thee'rt learning. But maybe I'll have a spell here and have a bit of fun with the other flatties. The word is that the humans will sort them all out before next winter.'

'That's what old Reynard said from the start. Two winters was all he gave them.'

'Well, he'd know.'

As it turned out, Charley had no fun at all with the City foxes. The humans caught several of them, kept them for a long time, and then turned them loose wearing collars. Charley had already had word of Rudyard's exploit high up in the heron's nest.

122

'I reckon, pal,' Charley said, 'as I might learn a thing or two myself if I was to stop with thee and thy pals for a spell.'

Almost a year it was now since Bushtail and the rest had arrived to settle in the country and, for reasons far different from those he had expected, he was happier than he had ever been in his life. Life was not at all like Ranter and Herman had said it would be. It was far, far better. It was what he knew in his heart the life of a fox should be. Redvers and Rudyard, too, were really happy, and Tinks and a few others seemed to have settled just as well. And now here was this new companion to make life even more interesting for a while.

Wanderer though he called himself, Charley was companionable in many ways and, for weeks throughout the summer, he would turn up occasionally and go exploring with Bushtail. There was no need for him to tell Bushtail about the big machines with which the humans came when it was time to cut the long grass and the corn. He had learned that lesson the hard way when poor old Rusty had been shot. But there were still many other ways in which he still had much to learn, and Charley was happy to teach him.

More and more as he had lived in the country, Bushtail had begun to understand how much he had lost through having been born in the City. He had seen already that fox cubs had to be taught by their mothers, so his mother had only been able to teach him how to live in the City. On top of that there had been all that foolish nonsense with Ranter and Herman about the constitution and all the rest of it, so it was small wonder that his knowledge of the country and its ways had been so limited. Still, he had learned a great deal, and now there was Charley who proved to be a good teacher.

The first trick Charley taught him was how to unroll and eat a hedgehog. Prickly things they were when they were curled up, but tasty indeed once they had been opened out.

Better than that, though, was the way Charley had of attracting some of the other stupid creatures. Out into a field he would go early in the morning and dance up and down, and jump about in circles, until some bird or stoat or rabbit would come close enough to see what was happening, and then Charley would pounce.

One fine morning they saw a falcon take a fat pigeon in full flight and Charley said, 'Now then, pal. Follow me.'

As the falcon glided down with its heavy prey and came to land, Charley pounced. To defend herself the falcon had to release the pigeon and, whilst she was trying to do battle with Charley, Bushtail made off with the pigeon. There had been no need for Charley to tell him.

So the summer passed and no word had there been from Charley for many days until Bushtail came upon a posting to say he had gone on his way. The word was that he would be back later on and mind for Bushtail to put in a good word for him with young Tinks because he definitely had ideas in that direction.

Harvest time came then, and several of Chopsy's members were caught in the corn fields when the humans came with their great machine going round and round until there was no place for a foxt to go, apart from making a dash for it and being shot as likely as not. And that was what happened to Chopsy himself, as well as the fools who were with him, according to the news item left by Blinker.

It was about this time, too, that some of the Chopsies were caught by the humans and released later on with collars on them. At first this was a cause for much concern, and more than one fox left news items at the old tree stump, as well as at other familiar posting places. They remembered only too well their fears and what agitation there had been when Herman had first appeared wearing his collar with the device in it. Reynard, however, was not unduly concerned and, if anything, was optimistic and advised patience. The humans were still paying regular visits to what had now become known amongst the foxes as Rudyard's tree in the fond belief that they were still tracking the movements of the late Comrade Herman.

'If we could handle that one,' Reynard said, 'we shouldn't have too much trouble with these others for all. But with a bit o' luck I reckon as the humans'll do the job for us.'

Reynard's wisdom had never been in question, and his reasoning in this case was simple. They would need to be watchful, he said, but they had to remember that the foxes with collars were not country foxes, and any day now the humans would be out with the young hounds, teaching them how to hunt and for them to learn how to kill. They would be the humans, just a few of them, who came without all the others in their bright coats, and it gave the vixens a chance to teach their cubs a thing or two as well, before they finally went out on their own in life. This year, Reynard said, it would have to be a pretty daft cub to get himself killed, with so many of these fools from the City about the place, with or without their collars.

It was a little bit later than this when they had arrived from the City the previous year, and Bushtail rememberd how Reynard had said at the time how lucky they had been, especially the younger ones, not to have arrived earlier when the humans had been out with the young hounds.

It happened sooner than they had expected or could have hoped. The next morning was crisp and clear and there was a message from Blinker that the humans were on their way. Every day for three days they came, and not a single country cub was killed. But by the time the few humans and the young hounds had finished, not a single fox wearing a collar remained alive and, according to the news items being left at the various posting places, no more than two or three of the other City foxes had survived.

Reynard had said originally that the City foxes who continued to live according to their City ways would be lucky to survive the second winter. In the event, they had not lived long enough to see it. In one way or another, Reynard reckoned, between the shooting and the dogs at harvest time, and then the young hounds soon after, the humans had done rather well by them.

On these occasions there had been none of the humans waving their flags to add to the excitement, and there had been no sign of those who had the things on their ears, and for putting to their eyes, and for making pictures. But some of them still paid regular visits to Rudyard's tree, so maybe they were content with that.

Chapter 19

AND REDVERS CAME HOME

That night as the moon rose, Charley came again. Blood red was the moon that night, red as the coat of Redvers, Charley said, and troubled was Charley because, of all the foxes he could have met, Redvers was the first. And that, Charley said, was a sign, for red was the moon, and red was the coat of Redvers, and red was the blood that would flow.

Charley spoke his strange gipsy words then, which none of them could understand, and he left other words at the tree stump to say that Redvers would surely die, and then he went on his way.

Redvers, wise and philosophical as ever, was none too distressed at word of Charley's premonition. He had enjoyed himself since coming from the City and was glad he had made the big decision to stay. It had been a good summer, they had done good work in helping the more sensible of the City foxes to adapt to their new life, and it had been great fun, and richly satisfying, getting rid of Ranter and Herman and some of those who had for so long led them astray in the City and had hoped to do the same in the country.

But there was a touch of winter in the air these days as the autumn leaves fell from the trees, and more than once of late Redvers had felt his age. On two occasions he had pounced on a rabbit and missed, and there were other similar little happenings which made him realise that his reactions were becoming slower. One night he would not be there to see the moon rise. That was a fact of life he had always accepted, he said to Bushtail, and Bushtail recalled that more than once Redvers had said that when his time came there was only one way he would want to go. And Bushtail said to himself that if Charley's wild gipsy prophecy proved to be true, then Redvers would have his wish.

Even so, the thought made Bushtail sad. Redvers had turned out to be a good companion, so much wiser and far-seeing than those who had derided him back there in the City. Not for the first time, Bushtail felt a twinge of shame that he himself had been one of them. Still, that was in the past, and none of the foxes now had a better understanding of the great part old Revers had played in bringing them safely to their journey's end.

For some days Bushtail was ill at ease, and little heart did he have for hunting by night. No sign had there been of the humans since the few of them had come with the young hounds to hunt the cubs, but they came at last in their great numbers wearing their bright clothes and, as Rudyard said, even a fox as short-sighted as Blinker could see them even if they hadn't been able to smell them or hear them. But it was the scent of them Blinker had first. Downwind he was, on a clear day, with a breeze coming from where the sun had risen, which every fox knew was not in favour of the hounds, and he passed on the word.

The foxes had no code in life other than a firm belief that life was a matter of every fox for himself. Yet now, so high was their regard for Redvers, and so deep an impression had Charley's prophecy made on them, that there was an unspoken feeling that they must do something other than save their own skins on this day. If they could contrive to lead the humans with their great hounds to be the death of Ranter, then it should not be beyond their wit to lead them away to save the life of Redvers. There was no need for any great plan. All it needed was for each of them to take up a little of the running.

Rather later than expected the first hounds came, and it was not until the following night that the reason became known, when a news item was left at the old tree stump to say that the hounds had found the last two stragglers of Chopsy's foxes and had spent a little time before they had caught and killed them. So it was afternoon before the hounds picked up the scent of Trotwood, and he led them a merry chase before Blinker took up the running. Then it was Bushtail and then Rudyard, and the foxes were satisfied that the humans would be well pleased because, even in such poor conditions for scent, hardly a check was there all afternoon.

But it was at this point that things went wrong, and Bushtail realised that they should perhaps have had a plan after all. They had not even thought to consult Reynard. Without warning, young Redvers appeared from nowhere, a great shout went up from one of the humans, and Bushtail knew a feeling of terrible despair. Herman had told them that there had been talk amongst the humans about the sighting of a fox with the dark red coat and the distinctive marking of Redvers' tail with its white tip and the dark ring round it, and some of the humans had said that long ago there had been foxes of such colour and markings in those parts. No wonder they were so excited as the hounds gave tongue.

Young Redvers, full grown now, made a handsome sight as he raced for the woods, but the hounds began to close on him, and Bushtail wondered whether Charley's prophecy could just as easily have applied to the son as to the father, and no doubt Tinks, too, would be sad and troubled.

And then, with the leading hound close upon him, young Redvers lost his head and jumped up to the lowest branch of a tree, as he had seen the great Rudyard do so recently. And, just as Rudyard had done, he began to climb. But these were different humans this time. Not content would they be to stand and look and listen.

The last rays of the blood red sun were going down beyond the hill when a strange thing happened. There was a glint of red reflected from the coat of the handsome fox that walked proudly out from the copse not fifty yards from where the humans were gathering. For moments there was a stunned silence and then the tree was forgotten and old Redvers gave them as good a run as his age allowed.

Well, Bushtail thought, that was the way he had said he wanted to go, and he had said he believed that his time could not be far off.

The horses, strung out, and some of them blowing hard, were plodding homewards, the hounds, panting and well

128

satisfied, just ahead of them. The humans, too, looked as if they had had enough for one day.

In the failing light a fox crossed in front of them, but they saw enough of him before he disappeared into the copse to note his colouring and his markings. A handsome young specimen he was, with a rich red coat and a white tip to his tail. Round the white tip there was a distinctive dark ring.

And the humans knew for sure, as Reynard and the other country foxes had known for a long time, that Redvers had come home.

Chapter 20

EPILOGUE

There is an urgent need for more meaningful funding in support of vital research into the life and habits of the fox.

This was the clear message to emerge from a Press Conference this week when Dr Des Ragwort, Chief Scientific Adviser to the Department of Interpretive Literature at the Ministry of Changing Patterns in Rural Living, presented an interim report on the latest findings of what is expected to be in depth research into the changes in vulpine behaviour.

The full text of the statement gives details of the research carried out to date which, said Dr Ragwort, is all that has been possible given the appalling lack of financial resources so far made available in support of this vital work.

'The interest of the Department,' states the report, 'was first alerted by stories that foxes had moved into certain localities in some numbers and in a hitherto unencountered behavioural pattern. For reasons which all interested parties will readily understand and hopefully accept, it is not intended at this stage to identify the area of these developments since it is important to discourage the unthinking and less knowledgeable members of the public from intrusion into such a sensitive area of scientific study in the field.

First sightings suggested that the newcomers were probably of the Common Fox species (*Vulpes vulpes*). The more experienced observers, however, suspected that some of them could possibly be of the Red Fox species (*Vulpes fulva*). In view of this divergence of expert opinion it was decided to call in the renowned EC taxonomist, Professor Nic Balonius. From the Professor's initial observations he considered it possible that the dominant species was possibly the Central European form (*Vulpes vulpes crucigera*). It is, however, accepted by taxonomists generally that there is little to distinguish between *Vulpes vulpes crucigera* and the Scandinavian form (*Vulpes vulpes vulpes*) which is known to occur in Scotland. It was, therefore, decided to initiate closer research and, as a result of this work, a most exciting discovery was made.

Professor Balonius and Dr Ragwort have now been able to identify a new species which is either the City Fox (*Vulpes urbanus*) or the Town Fox (*Vulpes oppidarius*). The possibility of a mutant cannot at this stage, and in the absence of further substantial funding, be entirely discounted.

The first step was to use a self-locking snare which facilitated the capture of one of these foxes which, in spite of the legendry cunning of the fox, proved to be remarkably simple. This specimen was then fitted with a collar, impregnated with a microchip containing a code which could be read by a telescopic scanner from a considerable distance.

A most interesting observation was that, from the outset, it was evident that this fox had no fear of humans and adapted readily to the surroundings in which it was kept and to the food which it was given. Its general behaviour suggested strongly that, given a correct and understanding approach by caring humans, foxes as a species could easily be domesticated to make delightful pets. This thesis was substantially confirmed when the captured fox, upon being released into the wild, returned after a few days and continued to follow this behavioural pattern on further occasions.

At this point in our work there was a most unfortunate development. People who no doubt meant well, and whose actions might possibly have been acceptable on other occasions, not knowing of the importance of the work in which we were involved, arrived with a vanload of foxes collected from the City and released them in the sensitive area of our research, thus confusing still further an already confused pattern, as well as attracting the attentions of those who would assuredly destroy the released foxes. This, some of the farmers immediately set out to do. Unquestionably because of this activity, the fox we had released did not return, and there was a clear signal that it had gone to earth and was not emerging.

When there had been no change in the situation for several days, the decision was taken to ascertain the cause of this behaviour. The fox had been identified as a male of the species so there was no question of its being with young. Investigation established that the fox had gone to ground in what was evidently a badger set of considerable depth, and this had the effect of nullifying the operation of the tracking device with which the fox had been fitted. Regrettable though it was, therefore, it was reluctantly decided that, for the sake of scientific knowledge and enlightenment, the fox would have to be dug out, even though this might mean disruption of the badgers which were not in any case the subject of our work.

Word of this operation would unfortunately seem to have been passed to a group of people who have been much in evidence in the countryside recently in their efforts to disrupt the activities of those who hunt foxes by way of sport. It is no purpose of this report to express an opinion on this emotive issue, our concern being entirely with scientific study, but it has to be stated that when these same people came with their banners and shouting obscenities it was embarrassing and disruptive in the extreme. Whilst it is fully appreciated that living on State Benefit, as many of them are, they need the extra money which they are paid for these activities, it is singularly unfortunate that they are completely incapable of listening to reasoned explanations of the nature and importance of the work which is being done. It must also be said that it was a matter of regret that some of the foxhunting fraternity, whilst taking no part in these offensive demonstrations, stood by and looked on with ill-concealed hilarity.

A most depressing result of this activity, however, was the fact that it made the foxhunting people, and indeed many others who are no friends of the fox, fully cognisant of the whereabouts of large numbers of the community of foxes it was our wish and earnest intention to study.

The decision having been taken, in view of this most undesirable and ill-informed interference, to abandon any thought of digging, it came as an interesting development a few nights later when it was ascertained that the fox had again emerged from its earth.

It is at this point that we have to report on one of the most exciting developments we have experienced, and it emphasises yet again, if there are still any to be found who would doubt it, the benefit to our understanding accruing from the development of sophisticated scientific instruments, and the urgent need for adequate funding to enable this important work to continue.

Being once more in the open air, the microchip was again emitting a clear signal, and this led us to some high trees on the river bank where there was a heronry with upwards of twenty pairs. To our astonishment, the fox was now comfortably settled in a heron's nest. At first, because the agitation amongst the herons was pronounced and noisy, we supposed this to be an intrusion, although we had reason to question this at a later stage of our observations. It was perhaps a little frustrating that, because of the large sticks of which the nest was made, it was not possible for the telescopic scanner to home in on the microchip, but this was not considered to be of vital importance since the fox was clearly visible. His head and his tail were both seen from time to time as he moved about in the nest, several good pictures were taken, and excellent sighting made possible by means of the binoculars.

Our efforts at observation were further rewarded later in the day by the presence of a most handsome vixen and her litter of half-grown cubs. They remained in the area for so long that they were clearly no strangers to it but, although we searched thoroughly, we completely failed to find any sign of a den or earth. Long before evening the herons had quite settled, and this led us to the conclusion that their original agitation had been caused by some other intrusion than that of the fox.

Although we continued with our observations long after the herons and their young had left the trees, we found no sign of a den or earth over a wide area, and yet there was indisputable evidence of vulpine presence and much activity, especially near and around the base of the tree which contained the nest. From this we could only deduce that the fox was leaving and returning during the hours of darkness. Due to the unfortunate underfunding of the project it was not possible to watch both by day and night, apart from which, in the absence of a sorely needed infra red scanner, the darkness imposes certain limitations on the efficacy of the equipment so far available.

Encouraged by what we had thus far been able to accomplish we took six more foxes, again with much greater facility than we would have expected, and fitted them with collars. We kept them confined for some time and weighed and measured them, as well as observing and recording certain patterns of behaviour, which will form the basis for certain scientific papers at a later date when adequate resources for the funding of this most important project have hopefully become available.

For whatever reason the response of these six foxes to human presence was somewhat different from that of the first fox to have been taken. What their reaction on being released into the wild would have been will never be known, however, because, the day after their release, the huntsmen went out cubbing with the young hounds, and all six foxes were killed, along with most of those whose movements we had planned to study. Three of the collars were recovered, but so far it has not been possible to take any more foxes alive.

At this point we can do no more than postulate on certain theories which present themselves, without any firm foundation in fact, and we emphasise that they should in no way be taken as positive conviction. At the same time, we cannot help but draw attention to the possibility of the overall effect of the ozone layer and global warming, which has been suggested by the uncharacteristic behaviour of the foxes which it had been hoped to study had not so many factors conspired against our best endeavours.

It is doubtful whether many, if indeed any, of this group of foxes now remain, other than those in the area of the heronry. We are satisfied beyond reasonable doubt that the fox carrying our collar is not the only one in the vicinity, and it is interesting to note that a young fox with a rich red coat and a white tip to its tail, with a distinctive black ring round it, has several times been observed. Whether this fox and any or all of the others have also taken to the trees it is impossible to say. The trees are too slender to take the weight of any humans who would be capable of climbing them, and there can be no question of cutting them down as they are in an an area which has been designated both an ESA and an SSSI. It is also too early as yet, and the evidence is too inconclusive, to suggest that another mutant of the species, such as the Heron Fox (*Vulpes ardea cinerea*) could be developing, but such a possibility cannot be discounted.

Meanwhile, watch is being kept at the site and will continue as long as funding remains available.'

Ends